MORE THAN A MATCH

As well as novels, Mark O'Sullivan has written
poetry, short stories and radio drama.
More Than A Match *is his third book for young*
people. His first novel, Melody for Nora, *won the*
Bisto Book of the Year Eilís Dillon Memorial Award,
and was shortlisted for the Reading Association of
Ireland Award.

With his wife Joan and daughters Jane and Ruth,
Mark O'Sullivan lives in Thurles,
Co. Tipperary.

For my parents

By the same author:
MELODY FOR NORA (Wolfhound Press 1994; reprint 1995)
WASH-BASIN STREET BLUES (Wolfhound Press 1995)

MORE THAN A MATCH

Mark O'Sullivan

WOLFHOUND PRESS

Reprinted 1998
First published 1996 by
WOLFHOUND PRESS Ltd
68 Mountjoy Square
Dublin 1

Wolfhound Press receives financial assistance from the Arts Council/ An Chomhairle Ealaíon, Dublin.

British Library Cataloguing in Publication Data
A catalogue record for this book is available from the British Library

ISBN 0-86327-496-X

Cover illustration: Angela Clarke
Cover design: James Carr
Typesetting: Wolfhound Press
Printed in the UK by Cox & Wyman Ltd., Reading, Berks.

CHAPTER 1

For two weeks, since the end of the school term, the summer sky had offered nothing but rain. Even today, when the sun had at last found a way to shine, there were clouds – and with each one Lida Hendel was reminded of Ginny Stannix. Clouds or no clouds, it was impossible to forget about Ginny when Mags Campion was around.

'She's brilliant,' Mags repeated for the umpteenth time on their long walk to the tennis club grounds.

The prospect of finally getting in some practice for the Junior Tennis Championship had lifted Lida's spirits for a while from the unhappiness in her home. Now, however, she'd begun to drift into a petulant, teeth-gritting silence.

'She's Schools Champion of Munster,' Mags added. 'She even has her own court on the lawn in front of her house.'

Lida grabbed her racket in both hands and squeezed hard. She stared at its frayed timbers as they passed over Blackcastle Bridge and wished she had the courage to fling it into the waters below and face the consequences.

Soon, her anger turned from Mags to her own father and his refusal to buy her a new racket. She was tired of making excuses for him, of trying to understand and humour him as her mother continued to do. It wasn't their fault that his dream had been laid waste. Why should they all have to suffer?

'You're very quiet in yourself,' Mags said.

With her red hair swept back tightly from her chubby face, for all her heavy awkwardness Mags might have passed as a ten-year-old. Though Lida was smaller and much leaner, her dark sallow features added a good two years to her fourteen. She wondered now if she should try, just one last time, to explain to Mags what was really on her mind.

'It's not fair,' her friend declared. 'Imagine having your own tennis court. God!'

Her tone was so peevish, so utterly silly that Lida knew she could never get Mags to understand.

'Anyway,' Mags shrugged, 'she's probably real snobby. Real ... serious, like.'

Lida suspected that Mags thought her the 'serious' type too. Only last week they'd had a row over playing 'shop' at Mags's house. In the end, however, Lida had given in and acted out the part of an irritated customer – not too difficult a role, given her foul humour on the day. Then again, Mags was her only friend and Lida imagined she would do anything to protect that friendship.

For the most part that was easy enough to do. Mags had a softness, a vulnerable nature that made Lida want to defend her from the many cruel remarks about her size. Yet Lida wasn't aware that Mags was sensitive to things she said, too. Or rather to the way she sometimes spoke, her hint of a German accent often seeming harsh and cutting – as it did right now.

'Forget about Ginny,' Lida said as she looked up at the heavy-laden sky. 'It's going to rain again soon, so let's make the best of it.'

At the green-painted, wooden pavilion with its covered veranda, Lida was delighted to find that they were the first pair to arrive. That meant they could use the main court and wouldn't have to struggle on the uneven surface of 'the Pit', the second court out behind the club building.

Better still was the fact that the club secretary, Mrs Mackey, was nowhere to be seen. Mrs Mackey had never forgiven Lida for beating her daughter, Mary, in the final the year before, and took every opportunity to avenge the slight on her family's pride by her tenant's daughter.

Though she was anxious to get right into trying some serves, Lida let Mags go first. The big girl's efforts were as wayward as ever. Keeping patience with her friend became more difficult by the minute as she chased misplaced shots into the lane beyond the court and onto the veranda of the pavilion. One particularly spectacular effort soared above the pavilion and into the Pit beyond.

'God, I'm useless,' Mags laughed.

'You're not concentrating, Mags,' Lida said, but Mags only giggled and let fly with another erratic swing.

When Lida's turn came to serve she was surprised at how quickly she got into her stride. This had always been the best part of her game. Nothing came close to the delicious feeling that shot through her as her racket met the ball in mid-air and she pounced forward to watch the white pellet swerve viciously towards its target. Mrs Mackey had her own view of Lida's merciless service shots.

'Girls,' she'd often said, 'shouldn't serve like that. It's not *ladylike*.'

Right now Lida didn't care about that sour-faced woman with her lipsticked mouth screwed tightly in a permanent state of outrage. For the moment she didn't care about anything. Not her father's meanness, nor her mother's unwillingness to challenge him. Even the plans of her older brother, Tommy, didn't bother her – plans that would surely lead to even more misery in their troubled house.

As Mags leapt away fearfully from each wicked serve, Lida became more and more lost in the passion of forgetting.

Her friend was tiring quickly and, finally, couldn't get out of the way of yet another lethal shot. The ball bounced a few feet in front of her and ricocheted into her stomach. She dropped to her knees as if she'd been gunned down and forced a pair of enormous tears from her eyes.

'Why do you have to be so ...' she moaned, 'so rough?'

'Rough'! The very word brought Lida back to the core of her unhappiness. If even her closest, her only friend saw her as nothing but a mean-spirited ruffian, was it perhaps true what she'd always suspected of herself? Did her true nature spring from the floodwater coursing of German blood in her veins? The same blood that had enriched the cruel hearts of the Nazis in the war which had ended only three years before?

Her racket felt like a revolver in her hand. She tossed it aside and went to Mags who, by now, was already smiling her broad, innocent smile.

'I'm sorry,' Mags apologised, 'I didn't mean to say that. You're just too good for me.'

'No, I'm not.'

'You know you are,' Mags insisted, raising her large frame a little unsteadily. 'If anyone can beat that snotty Stannix one, it's you.'

'Maybe if I had a better racket,' Lida said gloomily.

'You could always use mine.'

They both laughed as Lida dusted down her friend's blouse. Mags's racket was an even greater wreck than Lida's. Now they played from baseline to baseline and Lida touched out shots gentle enough for Mags to return. At least, she meant them to be gentle.

Mags, however, was struggling with the simplest lob and their rallies were annoyingly short. There was no chance to get into any rhythm of play and soon Lida was wishing they could just leave it. Her thoughts were back where she didn't want them to be, in that island of foreignness and despair that was No. 12 Garravicleheen.

She remembered her last futile attempt to tell Mags what lay at the root of her present misery. They'd just been to the Stella Cinema and Lida was certain that her friend's silence had something to do with what they'd just seen. Before the 'big picture' a newsreel had been shown. All the horror of a Nazi death camp had been made real before their eyes, with its sickening pile of fleshless, shaven-headed corpses.

As they'd walked home through the quiet, dark streets, Lida had launched into a tortuous explanation of her father's past. In the end, Mags had merely been confused and Lida herself was left feeling worse than when she had begun. For all its complications the story was, in the end, just another sad tale of how a man's life can be utterly changed by the huge forces of history over which he has no control.

Hendel was indeed a German name. There was no escaping the fact. However, there was more to it than that. Lida's father, Josef, had in fact been born in what was now Czechos-lovakia. His parents were German and had gone there to work on the estate of a German aristocrat. This was in the years before Czechoslovakia gained its independence.

Though German was the language of his home and school, Josef, in time, came to regard himself as a loyal Czechoslovak, proud of that country's achievements in the years after 1918 when it had become an independent state.

Josef's father came into possession of a small farm in the province of Moravia in 1919. Later that same year, Josef's mother died; a slight, frail woman of thirty, she'd been unable for the hard work required to eke out a living from farming.

Three years later, Josef left the farm near the small village of Palau to work in a sugar factory some eighty-five miles away. Very soon his father had married Frieda Bleimen, a widow with a son of Josef's age.

In 1925, as Josef laboured in the factory at Uherske Hradiste, his father met with a horrific accident. While he lay dying, Frieda persuaded him to leave the farm to her own son. When Josef was told of this, he vowed that one day he'd buy his own piece of land, and though only seventeen, began to save the little he could afford.

Soon he met Anna, who became his wife in 1930. His savings didn't last long in the first year of their marriage. When his son Tomas was born in 1931, he had almost given up on his promise to himself.

However, in that very year he and several others took up an offer to come to Ireland and help in the setting up of a sugar beet industry. The pay would be many times more than what it had been in Uherske Hradiste. His dream of making enough to buy his own place was possible again.

Early in 1932, Josef and his wife and child made the long journey by train from Moravia to Prague and on through Germany and Belgium. From Belgium they crossed the North Sea and by the Straits of Dover reached England. There they boarded another train, passed through London and on across the breadth of Britain to Holyhead. Another torrid sea-journey awaited and when they'd reached Dun Laoghaire, it was to meet a final train that would take them to Tipperary. Three days in all they travelled until they stepped out weary but excited into the small, grey, rain-soaked town on a February morning.

From the start they lived frugally, saving every penny. Lida, when she was born in 1934, was fitted out with her brother's baby clothes and as she grew, her mother knitted and sewed every last thing she ever wore. Nothing was bought that couldn't be made by their own hands.

By 1938 Josef had achieved his ambition, buying an old

farmhouse and twelve acres of vineyard through a friend back in Moravia. When the deeds to his little kingdom came in the post Josef Hendel was the happiest man alive. The preparations for their return began in earnest.

Then, as it had done for countless families, troubled times changed the course of the Hendels' lives. The evil ambitions of one man destroyed the dreams of many. That man was Adolf Hitler.

As Josef Hendel worked through the last months of his contract in Ireland, Hitler's armies were on the move. From the beginning, the Nazi leader had his sights set on the countries surrounding Germany. Painstakingly, he set about undermining Czechoslovakia's independence. Under the infamous Munich Agreement he was given control of those parts of the country which had a majority of Germans over the local population.

Josef delayed his return, not wanting to be party to this take-over. Within a year Adolf Hitler was in Prague with his troops. Czechoslovakia's freedom was at an end and World War Two soon began.

When the conflict finally ended, all Germans and those of German descent were expelled from the country by an angry Czech people. Now, three years later, the Communists had seized power and had already begun to take over all privately owned land. Lida's father would never set foot on his twelve acres, or brush the cobwebs from the empty farmhouse to begin a new life there.

All that was left to him were the useless deeds to the land and an old photograph of the house. However, even as his dream faded over the last ten years, he had insisted on continuing to live simply, adding more and more to his savings. It had become such a way of life for all of them that Lida had accepted it without question.

Only when she became friendly with Mags, almost a year ago now, did she begin to realise what she was missing. There were, in truth, very few girls in town whose parents could afford to indulge them as much as Mags Campion's did. Ration books were still very much a part of people's lives, though the shops were becoming better stocked, even with little luxuries – chocolate spread, bananas, oranges. Lida never tasted these delights except at Mags's house. Her friend's father was a senior clerk in the Munster and Leinster Bank and Mags was an only child.

A month rarely passed but Mags was fitted out with a new dress or coat or shoes. Every week she got a film magazine from the paper shop. She could have had a new tennis racket too but preferred to get clothes instead. Tennis wasn't important to her as it was to Lida. It was more a chore to be carried out on the insistence of her parents, so that she might 'mix with the right people'. The very foreignness that Lida so despised in herself made her an acceptable friend for Mags as far as her parents were concerned. The fact that Mr Campion was aware of Josef Hendel's considerable savings also helped to convince them.

The sacrifice of all these pleasures that Mags enjoyed might have been tolerable for Lida if it hadn't been for the dramatic downturn in her father's mood earlier in the year. That was when the Communists finally took control of Czechoslovakia and all hope of a reversal in his fortune was lost forever.

He would spend hours, as he'd done once again last night, in his room staring at the old photograph. He showed no interest in her tennis playing and hardly noticed her frustration as she sat watching the eternal rain that threatened to spoil her chances of winning the Junior Championship again.

Chasing a ball arching wildly from Mags's racket, Lida remembered what he'd said when she'd finally complained loudly about the weather a few days ago.

'*Du weiss nicht was Ärger ist, mein Kind.*'

You don't know what trouble is, child! There was no answer to that, or none that she had the courage to offer. Instead she cursed silently the fact that they always spoke German at home. She couldn't understand why he would want to use the language of those who'd destroyed his life. As for herself, having to speak German made her feel even more isolated at home than she did outside it.

Worse still, it made her feel unclean, reminding her that inside stirred the same brutishness that lay behind the atrocities of the Nazis. No matter how hard Lida tried to put it from her mind, her friend's accusation would not go away. Her shots were beginning to become vengeful again and she knew she'd better call a halt to their practice.

As if coming to her rescue, an impeccably polished blue Delage car eased its way along the grass-covered lane and stopped at the little wicket gate leading to the pavilion. The car, with its retractable brown leather hood, its two spare tyres neatly fastened together at the rear, and its distinctive oval insignia on the gleaming front grille, was a familiar sight around town, standing out colourfully among the few sombre black vehicles on the quiet streets.

At the wheel was Hubert Stannix, Ginny's uncle, known to all as a strange, eccentric type. His oddness was put down to his war-time experiences in the British Army. His brother Robert, Ginny's father, had, it was said, died in his arms on a battlefield in France in 1941. Though not yet forty, his scarecrow mop of hair was already quite grey. He never ventured beyond the leafy bounds of Stannix House except to chauffeur his sister-in-law, Rose, and his niece around.

In the passenger seat was Mrs Mackey, the club secretary, wearing a brown tweed suit that matched her dyed brown hair perfectly. Her powdered face showed every sign of her sheer ecstasy in being granted the privilege of sitting in the Stannix car. Behind her sat the girl who threatened to make Lida's life outside as miserable as her home life in that German-speaking bunker.

The same girl who had never condescended to play even once at the local tennis club. Why did she have to come now, when things were already unbearable for Lida? Why did she come now to steal the only thing that gave her any pleasure, any belief in herself? Her title: Junior Champion.

Ginny Stannix, elegant in her perfect whites, her short gold-blonde hair a perfect crown above the pale, regal face. The girl, Lida thought, who had everything, coming for more. The silver trophy on Lida's dresser came to mind, its tall ebony mounting studded with silver tabs, and on each tab engraved the year and the champion's name. She saw clearly the tab declaring, '1947 – Lida Hendel'.

And below, the dark space waiting for this year's flash of silver. . . .

CHAPTER 2

'Come on, Mags, try another serve.'

Lida was suddenly determined to hold on to the main court, even if it meant putting up with her friend's hopeless efforts. Even hitting the ball, however, was now a problem for Mags, what with Mrs Mackey and Ginny watching from the wicket gate. Her nervousness was infectious and soon Lida was making mistakes she never made with such frequency.

After the ball had once more struck the timber of her racket and screwed away she caught a glimpse of Ginny's face. She was sure that behind that smug grin lay surprise, even delight, at how poor a player this so-called Junior Champion really was.

'LIDA!' Mrs Mackey's voice crackled as it always did when she addressed her.

Chasing an unexpected return from Mags, Lida ignored the prim, straight-backed club secretary. She just about reached the ball but sent it crashing into the net.

'Dammit!' she grunted, and threw her racket on the ground.

'LIDA!' Mrs Mackey called out, aghast.

Perspiration trickled onto Lida's darkly arching eyebrows. She brushed back the wet, straggly fringe from her forehead and stared sullenly at the woman in the brown tweed suit.

'I won't have it,' Mrs Mackey cried. 'Rule 24:1(b) – court

etiquette. We do not throw tantrums.'

'I didn't throw a tantrum. I threw a racket.'

Ginny chuckled gracefully and Lida gave her an icy look. Only now did she see the two stylish rackets the girl was holding nonchalantly. She went and picked up her own shabby one but she wasn't about to give in. She grabbed the ball and stalked back to the end line. When she turned around she saw that Mags was already heading away to the pavilion.

'Mags! I'm not ... we're not finished yet.'

By now, Mrs Mackey was advancing across the court with mincing steps. Her shocking pink pout was trembling and her whole body seemed electrified.

'Really, Lida,' she whispered indignantly, 'what will Miss Stannix think of us? This club has a reputation to uphold and even as a junior member you have a duty to behave yourself.'

'You want me to clear off so snotty-pants over there can play, is that it?'

'Miss Stannix is the kind of member this club needs, and ...'

'And I'm not?'

'For heaven's sake, keep your voice down,' Mrs Mackey urged. 'Now, you've had plenty of time to practise on the main court and Miss Stannix has never played here so it's only fair that she ...'

'Fair? She's not even a member.'

'And if you keep carrying on like this, she'll never want to be.'

From behind the club secretary, Ginny appeared, an unruffled smile playing across her beautiful mouth.

'It's quite all right,' she said, very precisely. 'There's a second court, isn't there? I really don't mind where I play.'

Lida was incensed. It seemed to her that what Ginny meant was that no matter which court she played on, she would be equally unbeatable. Mrs Mackey held Ginny's arm gently and twisted her puckered face into a mask of wistful servility.

'You and I, my dear, will play on this court,' she said and, glancing at Lida, added, 'now.'

From the pavilion, Mags beckoned Lida with a concerned nod. There seemed no point in protesting any further. Mrs Mackey never gave way. With one last glare at the pair of intruders, Lida turned away and made for the pavilion.

'Excuse me,' Ginny called, just as Lida stepped from the short, springy turf of the court on to the rougher grass beyond.

Lida swivelled around sharply and noticed the look of quivering uncertainty on Mrs Mackey's face.

'I'm sorry,' Ginny continued politely, 'but we haven't been introduced.'

The club secretary raised her hands and joined them together as if in prayerful apology.

'Of course,' she cried, 'what was I thinking of?'

'Virginia Stannix,' the girl said and walked confidently towards Lida, offering a delicate, long-fingered hand.

Lida wiped her sweaty palms along her skirt and shook hands without feeling.

'Lida Hendel,' she said and it came out sounding like a challenge rather than an introduction.

'Lida!' Ginny smiled. 'Such a beautiful name. "Leda and the Swan". In Yeats's poem, you know?'

'No, I didn't.'

'We'll meet again, no doubt,' Ginny said.

'I suppose so.'

Though Mags stood only a short distance away, Lida thought she would never get to her side. She felt sticky and uncomfortable under the gaze of Mrs Mackey and the too-perfect girl. She stumbled foolishly on the gravel path leading to the wooden building and blushed deeply at her awkwardness.

'Goodbye, Lida,' Ginny called.

In her mind, Lida was crying out to the girl to stop looking at her, to stop making her feel so small and petty.

'Nice to meet you,' Ginny added as Lida reached Mags's side.

'I wish she'd shut up,' she whispered savagely. 'Little Miss Flippin' Perfect.'

'She's only trying to be nice,' Mags said.

'What did you go running off for,' Lida snapped, 'just because Mackey wanted to get rid of us?'

Mags's big innocent face paled.

'You were fed up of playing with me, anyway,' she said.

'No, I wasn't,' Lida answered, knowing Mags was right.

'Yes, you were,' Mags insisted. 'You think I'm a fool? Just because I'm so … clumsy and …'

'Mags, you're my best friend,' Lida pleaded. 'I don't think you're a fool.'

'But you know I'm clumsy. Everyone does.'

'Let's go home, Mags,' Lida said. 'We'll try again tomorrow. We're just out of practice, that's all. Talk about clumsy! I was so awful today, I couldn't move. I couldn't hit the ball, I …'

Lida talked and talked because there was no response from her friend. Nothing more than a downcast look. A fearful panic gripped her and when she stopped rabbitting on at last, she knew the reason for it.

'Are you coming?' she asked, but the question she was really asking was, 'Are you still my friend?'

There was no answer from Mags, just a slow shake of her head.

'But there's no one for you to play with here.'

'Somebody will come,' Mags muttered, never raising her eyes. 'I'll find somebody.'

Behind her the ball popped from racket to racket as Ginny and Mrs Mackey exchanged genteel shots. Lida went on her way, ignoring Ginny's pleasant nod as she passed by the main court. Once out of sight she broke into a half-trot and didn't stop until her hand touched the cold metal of the front gate at No. 12 Garravicleheen. But there was no peace or comfort to be found here.

Even as she opened the gate, the sounds of a heated argument reached her ears. Her father and Tommy were at each other's throats again. Sometimes Lida wished that her brother had no talent for music at all and no crazy ambition to build his life around it. However, she knew quite well that they would always find something to fight about, music or no music.

She turned the key and entered the narrow, dark hall-way of the small terraced house. Her father rented it from Seamus Mackey, a local shopkeeper and husband of her arch enemy, Mrs Mackey. Each time Lida stepped inside the front door she was filled with disgust that they had to be tenants of that woman.

Mr Mackey himself was a small, inoffensive man who never had a bad word to say about anybody. He would come quietly every Friday evening, collect what he was owed and leave just as quietly. However, on those Fridays when his wife called it was a different matter. She snooped around and made sarcastic comments on how they were keeping the place.

On the last few occasions she'd been, she'd dropped some very heavy hints about the state of the long stretch of garden out behind the house. When Lida's parents had moved in eight years before, the garden had been little short of a rubbish tip. In a matter of weeks her father had cleared the thicket of weeds and brambles, carted away tractor-loads of decaying waste and put some order on the chaos.

Directly behind the house, he set an area of lawn surrounded by a laurel hedge and dotted with shrubs and flowers. Further back, a little more out of sight each year as the hedges grew, a neat vegetable garden took shape and beyond, three apple trees stood, one of sweet Pippins, the others providing big dark green 'cookers'.

As the years passed and he spent more long hours at the factory, his wife took charge of the vegetables. The lawn and hedges, the shrubbery and flowers were in his care. He worked there late into the evenings when other men might have been resting after their day at the workplace.

However, his interest had waned of late and in February, when he should have been out helping his garden back to life after the winter, he was invariably in his room, brooding. The burst of new growth had gone completely unchecked in his part of the garden. Anna had enough to do to keep the vegetable garden in order. Josef didn't seem to notice or, if he did notice, he wasn't up to caring.

'Du darfst nicht gehen!'

He was bellowing now, at the top of his voice. You will not go where, Lida wondered? She thought about dashing straight up to her room and burying her head under the pillow as she often did when the rows began. She remembered the pale sad face of her mother and decided she couldn't leave her to deal with their relentless feuding alone.

'I've made up my mind,' Tommy countered, 'and I'm not changing it. I don't care what you say.'

The kitchen door trembled on its hinges as it always did when she opened it. Like everything else in this house it was on the point of falling apart. Inside, a miserable excuse for light leaked from the big bulb in its home-made cardboard shade. The kitchen was so dark they had to have the light on most of the time. Lida's mother sat at the table, her floury hands kneading the dough for her black bread. The Hendels never ate shop bread.

At opposite ends of the same table Tommy and his

father stood trying to shout each other down. This particular disagreement was one that Lida should have expected since Tommy had let her in on the secret he'd kept from his parents until this moment. As soon as she'd heard it, Lida knew it spelt more trouble.

For months now, even as he was studying for his Leaving Cert, Tommy had been rehearsing with a new dance band in town. Instead of going to his friend's house he would go every second night to the Confraternity Hall and play the piano and piano accordion with the other members of The Silver Sound.

When he'd told Lida about this venture she'd protested, pleading with him to wait at least until the exams were over. He'd agreed to miss rehearsals during the two weeks before they started, but now the real moment of crisis had come. The Leaving Cert was over. What Tommy regarded as his real life could begin.

The band were to play at their first dance tonight in Cashel, some twelve miles away. Tommy had just broken the news to his father. But he'd said more. He'd said he wanted to make a living from music.

'Music!' his father sniffed. 'Music won't put food on your plate.'

'It's what I want to do,' Tommy said. 'The only thing I want to do.'

'You will go to university and study to be an engineer just like we always planned.'

'Like *you* always planned, Papa!'

Their voices were almost at screaming pitch now and Lida knew what to expect next. They would fix each other with malicious glares, lower their tones and begin to spit out the most hurtful things they could conjure up. To Lida they were like two tall trees planted alongside one another in a forest. The storm of futile argument whipped their branches, their branches whipped each other mercilessly, uselessly, for neither of them would ever be moved from his fixed spot. As for Lida and her mother, they were like children lost in that same forest from which there seemed no escape.

'And these people, these so-called musicians, I know who they are and what they are. Layabouts, too lazy to work. They're not men at all.'

'You don't have to break your back in a factory to be a man.'

'Ger Kinsella,' Lida's father said, lingering drily over each syllable of The Silver Sound bandleader's name, 'an alcoholic waster from the slums of Dublin. And this is the kind of company you want to keep?'

'Maybe he's not afraid to enjoy himself,' Tommy muttered.

'What did you say?'

Anna Hendel looked up from the doughy mixture on the table. The hand wiping her wet brow left a white streak.

'Please,' she said firmly, hesitating a little between each word, 'Stop ... this ... bickering ... now.'

Her husband looked at her like a hurt child whose mother has taken sides against him. Tommy avoided her eyes altogether and Lida knew why.

'I'm sorry,' he told Anna. 'I should have told you, Mama.'

'But not me,' his father said bitterly. He left the kitchen, slamming the frail door behind him. Anna smiled sadly at her son and daughter. Lida wondered if she was wishing they were infants again, their troubles small and insignificant.

'Mama,' Tommy pleaded, 'it's what I want to do, you know that.'

Lida was shaking with temper, more angry with her mother than with either Tommy or her father.

'Why do you never get mad at him, Mama?' she asked. 'Why? He's making our lives miserable just because of that stupid old farm and ... and we have to live in this dump of Mrs Mackey's because he can't make up his mind to ...'

'That's enough, Lida,' her mother said. 'Your father will make the right decision when the time comes.'

'God, you're so flippin' patient.'

'Lida,' Tommy objected, 'mind what you're saying.'

'Ah, shut up,' she cried. 'You're nothing but a trouble-maker anyway.'

'Stop it,' her mother insisted. 'Do you want the neighbours to think we're always fighting?'

'Well we are, aren't we? And, anyway, if we got one of those new factory houses we wouldn't have to stay in this shed. I can hear Mrs Maher next door snoring every night, for God's sake.'

'Your father has another month to decide about taking one of those houses,' Anna told her. 'It's a big commitment. A lot of money is needed. Most of our savings, maybe.'

Tommy, tall and broad-shouldered and fair like his father, stood at the kitchen door shaking his head in exasperation.

'What,' he asked, 'is he saving for now? Doesn't he know as well as we do he'll never see Moravia again?'

'Do you have any idea what it costs to go to university?' his mother asked.

'But I don't want to go,' Tommy groaned, 'and besides, I don't believe he's hoarding his money for my sake. Do you?'

Anna made him no answer. She had a question of her own to ask.

'Are you going to Cashel?'

In spite of her annoyance with him, Lida was touched by his look of fierce regret.

'I don't want to hurt you, Mama. I don't want to hurt

anyone,' he said. 'I don't have a choice. This is something I have to do.'

He went outside to the hallway and they waited to hear the front door close out. When it did, Lida placed her hand on her mother's shoulder and her mother took it and pressed it against her flushed cheek.

CHAPTER 3

'Are you awake, Lida?'

It was three o'clock in the morning but it seemed to Lida that she'd been sleeping only a very few minutes. She'd been tossing and turning and worrying about what was to become of her family. Now, Tommy's eager whisper had sent her spinning from her forgotten dream world and she despaired of finding any rest that night.

'I am now,' she said drily.

'Sorry, Lida,' he said. 'I just had to talk to somebody.'

Tired as she was, she could feel his enthusiasm fill the confined space of her bedroom. As always, when they spoke together, it was in English, which lent an air of conspiracy and defiance to their every conversation.

'I've never felt anything like it. I was shaking,' Tommy went on, still shaking. 'I really thought I wouldn't be able to play a note but I knew I had to. And I did. You should've heard us, Lida.'

'Took you long enough to get home.'

If Tommy was unhappy at her reaction it didn't show. She might as well not have been there, he was so intent on reliving his first stage appearance.

'It's nothing like playing on your own,' he told her. 'Playing with a band you feel you're part of something and when it comes right! Like when we played "In the Mood". I felt like I was floating above the stage and I could see the lads and myself too belting it out on the last chorus and it was … I don't know … magical!'

Though she couldn't see his face clearly in the darkness, she guessed it must be transfixed. She was glad that he couldn't see her either. If he had he would have noticed a grim, distant look about her. For a moment she thought she could understand the real reason for her father's anger towards Tommy.

Her brother knew what he wanted from life and had now taken the first step in the direction he'd planned out for himself. Nothing, it appeared, no outside force, no matter how great, would stop him. It was perhaps natural for her father to be simply jealous of his son. Right now, Lida certainly was.

'It must have been nice for you,' she said.

Still, Tommy wasn't to be put off. He stretched himself across the foot of her bed unaware of the fact that he was squashing her toes.

'Do you mind,' she yelped, nudging him away and wishing she could kick him harder.

'Then I did a solo, French-style, on the piano accordion,' he continued. '"Flambee Montalbanaise". And the crowd! Cripes, they brought the house down. I was … I was …'

'Floating,' Lida yawned.

'Yeah, floating,' he said, his voice soft and mellow as if the music had entered his very soul and would ring for-ever in every word he spoke.

'I suppose Ger Kinsella was floating too,' she said, 'in a sea of beer.'

'Ger is all right. Maybe he drinks too much since the wife died but he's been good to me. He's ten years older than Papa but he's like a young fellow. At least he knocks a bit of crack out of life.'

'I'm tired,' she said, hoping he'd go.

Tommy raised himself from the bed and went to the

window on the other side of the room. He inched back the curtain and a bright shaft of moonlight lit up his features.

'While you were knocking a bit of crack out of life for yourself,' she told him firmly, 'I had to sit below in that dungeon of a kitchen and they never said a word to each other all night. He wouldn't even let me listen to the radio. I hate him. I hate him!'

'I'm sorry,' Tommy said, as if he'd only just become aware of her presence.

He came and sat beside her again. For a while he didn't speak. Lida thought he was probably having trouble thinking about anything other than himself and his music. It seemed to her that happiness was a purely selfish thing, a thing you could only get if you ignored the feelings of others.

'The sky is clear,' he said. 'You'll get plenty of practice in tomorrow.'

'It's all the same how much I practise,' she sighed. 'I can't beat Ginny Stannix with my crock of a racket.'

'Didn't you trounce Mary Mackey with that racket last year?'

'But it's falling apart, Tommy. It's like trying to play tennis with a fishing net.'

'There's nothing wrong with the racket,' Tommy insisted. 'The problem is Ginny, isn't it?'

'No, it's not.'

'If you get it into your head that you can't beat her, it won't matter what you play with.'

'Leave me alone,' she retorted. 'All you care about is your music.'

She pulled the sheet over her head and as he moved across to the bedroom door she muttered curses at him under her breath. He was probably right but that didn't make the truth any easier to bear. She was certainly letting Ginny's reputation get to her. After all, she'd never seen

the girl play except to exchange lazy strokes with Mrs
Mackey. Yes, Ginny was a schools champion, but did that
really mean anything? Was she perhaps just champion of
a bunch of prim snobs who were more interested in
sporting the right outfits than actually playing to win?

Whether Ginny was a good player or not, it was difficult
for Lida not to worry about this racket of hers. She'd been
using it for three years, ever since she'd taken up the game,
and even then it had been second-hand. Second-hand!
Third or fourth-hand more likely.

It occurred to her that she might actually go and smash
it to pieces and pretend a car had driven over it up at the
club. However, her father had grown so miserly that she
was afraid he might not replace it at all and decided against
the idea. She would have to make the best of what she had
and take every chance that came between the showers of
summer rain to sharpen up her game. Drifting finally to
sleep, she hoped Tommy had been right about tomorrow's
weather.

Early next morning, before she'd even opened her eyes,
Lida felt a pleasant warmth wash over her. Through a
chink in the curtain she caught a glimpse of the perfect
blue of the day. She was filled with an urgency that had
her springing from the bed, dressing quickly and racing
down the stairs before she was yet fully awake. Even in
the damp-smelling kitchen the sunlight seemed to reach
into corners it hadn't touched for years. Her mother's
mood was bright too, her whole being radiant with good
memories.

'On days like these Moravia is so beautiful,' she said.
'Your father and I, we'd climb to the old ruins on the hill
above the village, through the trees from one clearing to
the next until we reached the top. And the view! We could
see right across into Austria and your father would say

that if you climbed high enough above this world there were no borders, no limits to what you could do.'

It wasn't a morning for arguments. Lida resisted the temptation to ask her mother why she always had to look back to the past, as her father did. Wolfing down her breakfast she returned without delay to her room for her racket. Somehow it didn't seem half as rickety now and she laughed off her misgivings about it. A few minutes later she was on her way to Mags Campion's house, hoping her friend had woken with the same enthusiasm she had.

As she walked along through Garravicleheen she bounced the strings of her racket against the heel of her palm. A pleasant tension stirred in her and she felt the confidence that had been draining away return with every step.

Mags lived among a row of spacious, bay-windowed houses on the tree-lined mall. It was a bright, welcoming street and never more so than on that sunny morning. The usual pangs of envy Lida felt when approaching her friend's house were for once forgotten as she looked forward to really getting down to work on her game.

Mrs Campion, a much larger version of Mags, was as good-humoured as ever when she answered the front door. She brought Lida inside to the sitting room of the home that was like a doll's house. Mags hadn't gotten up yet but Lida didn't mind the wait, sitting comfortably in a sun-filled room and drinking tea from Mrs Campion's fragile bone china delph.

The sitting room couldn't have been more different from the dark cells of her own home. It was a little too fussily frilly for Lida's taste but it was still a delightful place to be.

From time to time, Mrs Campion would interrupt her steady flow of easy conversation and go to the sitting room door to call Mags. Lida wasn't surprised at Mags's slowness in coming down. Her friend wasn't the energetic type and though it was now almost ten o'clock, it would still be very early for her to be up and about – especially during holiday time.

'Maybe I should call back later,' Lida said, having finished a third cup of tea.

'Indeed you won't,' Mrs Campion declared. 'I'll go up this instant and get her out of it.'

Soon, Lida heard the hushed, insistent tones of Mrs Campion and the equally insistent murmurs of Mags. She was beginning to feel like an intruder. It was as if her very presence had upset the peaceful order of this pleasant haven. The voices upstairs seemed to bristle with an unexpected sharpness. In her hand the delicately etched tea cup tinkled tremulously on its matching saucer. She set them down carefully on the low table beside her and stood up as Mags and her mother descended the stairs.

'Here we are at last,' Mrs Campion beamed, filling the doorway with her great bulk. 'I'll leave you to it. I've so much to do and the house is in a terrible state.'

She moved away to reveal a sulking, sleepy-eyed Mags standing with her arms tightly folded across a long-sleeved nightdress that was at least two sizes too small for her. Mags pottered heavily into the sitting room and flopped into a chair by the window. Her eyes were firmly fixed on some distant point in the garden as she spoke.

'What time is it?'

'Just after ten,' Lida said. 'I thought you might be up since it was such a nice morning, you know?'

'Well, I'm up now,' Mags said.

Lida didn't sit down. Somehow she knew she'd be leaving soon – alone.

'I thought we might go up to the club and …'

Drawing up her feet wearily onto the chair Mags sighed deeply. She was still staring through the window.

'Not this morning, Lida,' she said. 'My legs are killing me after yesterday.'

'But we didn't play for long,' Lida objected; 'we didn't get a chance to.'

'I played some more after you went home.'

The truth was beginning to dawn on Lida, the answer to her next question clear in her mind before she spoke.

'Who did you play with?' she asked as brightly as she could.

'Virginia Stannix,' Mags told her. 'Ginny. She was ever so nice.'

Lida wished Mags would at least look in her direction and see the evidence of her pain.

'She was so patient,' Mags added. 'She didn't mind when I missed the ball or hit it up in the clouds.'

'I don't mind when you do that either.'

'That's not how it seems to me,' Mags said evenly.

'What do you mean?'

Mags turned her head slowly from whatever it was she'd been gazing at outside.

'You know well what I mean,' Mags said. 'You think I'm not good enough for you to play with.'

'I never said any such thing.'

'You don't have to say it, it's sticking out a mile. Just because you're … you're different, you think you're great. You think the rest of us are just here for you to push around.'

By now, Lida's apprehensiveness was changing to a dry bitterness. She felt she was making little of herself in her efforts to keep on the right side of her 'friend'. In any case, how deep did that friendship really go if Mags could speak to her like this?

'It's not my fault if you're too …' (she was going to say,

'Too fat and lazy,' but stopped herself) 'too slow and you keep ballooning the ball all over the place.' Mags smiled at her coldly. She eased herself from her chair and went to the door, holding it open for Lida. Grabbing her racket from the floor, Lida brushed past her and strode out into the hall. From the kitchen door Mrs Campion gaped at her as she snatched open the front door. Taking one last look around the lush-laced interior, Lida regarded the pair with a dismissive look.

'I suppose you both wear frilly knickers too,' she said and swept out by the flowery footpath.

The sunlight dappling through the trees on the mall held no pleasure for her now, no promise of better days. She wondered whether she'd bother going to the tennis club, afraid it would lead to more disappointment. Yet, surely someone would take pity on her and not leave her sitting alone in the pavilion.

Suddenly the idea of being pitied appalled her. She would survive on her own if that was how it had to be. She felt like a small animal who'd strayed into town from the wild – unwanted, even feared. A poor stray whose own fear and confusion is greater than that of those who flee from it.

In such a state of mind, the last person she needed to meet at the tennis club was Mrs Mackey. As she walked down the grassy lane she might have guessed that the club secretary was lying in wait for her, ready to pounce.

CHAPTER 4

'Lida Hendel!'

The boys playing on the main court stopped their game and looked from Mrs Mackey to Lida and back again. They grinned at each other and continued, their ears cocked for the war of words that was sure to erupt. Lida passed by the court looking frostily at the sniggering pair.

'LIDA!'

Mrs Mackey's cheeks had turned an unhealthy violet which no amount of face powder could cover up. She stamped her foot twice, three times on the veranda, until it seemed the whole pavilion was possessed by her rage. Lida approached her looking very calm, but inside she was gripped by a cold fury. She came to the foot of the steps leading to the timber frame building and leaned against the handrail there.

'You wanted to speak to me?' she asked sweetly.

'Ooooh, yes,' the club secretary cried, 'I certainly do.'

'About what?'

'Come into my office this instant.'

What Mrs Mackey called her 'office' was a small store room at the rear of the pavilion where she'd installed a chair, a desk and a filing cabinet filled with useless bits of paper. Lida had no desire to be hauled in there and made to stand while Mrs Mackey sat, as she always did, like a judge passing sentence on some miscreant.

'Whatever you have to say, you can say it here,' Lida told her.

'My office,' Mrs Mackey intoned, turning on her heel and entering the shadowy green interior of the pavilion.

Hesitating for a moment, Lida heard the boys on the main court whispering behind her back. She faced them with hands on her hips.

'What are you smiling at, spotty face?' she snapped.

'Hey,' one of them piped up, 'watch what you're saying.'

'Ah, go jump in the river,' she said and followed Mrs Mackey into her ridiculous little den.

As she'd guessed, her tormentor was already sitting pompously behind her desk, her over-sized spectacles balanced uncertainly like the scales of justice on her button nose. Before her was the book she referred to as her 'bible'. The rule book of the tennis club. Lida wondered why the woman bothered to open it since she seemed to know every page by heart.

'Not for the first time,' Mrs Mackey began, in a great effort at eloquence, 'I am impelled to remind you of Rule 24...'

'I know the rule,' Lida interrupted.

The spectacles dropped onto the open page as Mrs Mackey's nostrils widened and narrowed uncontrollably. She banged the desk with her fist and her knuckles met the sharp edge of a brass paperweight beside the rule book. Her scream silenced the echoes of voices from the courts outside.

'Are you all right?' Lida asked, secretly delighting in the woman's pain.

'Yes,' Mrs Mackey groaned, 'bruised inside and out from dealing with the likes of you but I'll ... I shall be fine. I'm quite sure I shall feel much better when I've finished with you.'

Whatever Mrs Mackey had in store for her, Lida knew

it was going to be more than a mere telling off.

'Members,' she read aloud, 'shall at all times observe the requisite standards of decorum in their general play and in all other activities whether of an official or social nature pertaining to their membership of the club.'

She closed the book and raised herself haughtily in her seat. Lida was surprised she didn't bless herself.

'Your behaviour yesterday and indeed just now – really, calling Dr Molloy's son such offensive names. Well, it's simply unacceptable.'

Continuing her lecture, Mrs Mackey listed a whole series of incidents going back over the three years since Lida had joined the club. Lida might have stood up for herself more vehemently if her attention hadn't been drawn from the woman altogether by a sheet of paper pinned to the noticeboard above her busily bobbing head. It contained the details of the draw for the first round of the Junior Championship.

'Furthermore,' Mrs Mackey droned on, 'and I'm not saying this because your opponent happened to be my daughter, but during last year's final you threw your racket on the ground twice, made five objections to my … to the umpire's decisions, shouted at my daughter … that is … your opponent on three separate …'

The print was large enough for Lida to read every name. She stared in disbelief as it became clear to her that she was once again being cheated by this vengeful woman. Twenty-eight competitors were listed. This meant that four players would be given byes into the next round. Normally the top players would be the ones to expect these. Ginny's name was among the four. Lida's wasn't.

'Why didn't I get a bye in the first round?' Lida asked, cutting Mrs Mackey off in mid-sentence. 'I'm the champion, for God's sake.'

'You haven't been listening to a word I've said,' Mrs

Mackey exclaimed. 'I haven't brought you in here to dis-
cuss the draw.'

'Why did Ginny get one and not me?'

'Miss Virginia Stannix to you,' the woman said with-
eringly. 'Only her friends call her Ginny.'

'Just because I beat your daughter, you're picking on
me.'

Surprised by Lida's directness, Mrs Mackey began
shuffling the book and the paperweight around the desk.
She made blustering, flustered noises that didn't quite
hide her obvious guilt.

'It was a perfectly fair draw,' she muttered, 'wit-
nessed by my dear husband and several other commit-
tee members.'

'Which ones?'

'I ... I can't quite remember but it doesn't matter and I'll
have you know that if these insinuations of yours are
repeated outside these four walls your suspension will be
even more severe.'

'My suspension?'

Lida held on to the edge of the desk to steady herself.
Mrs Mackey, avoiding her eyes, was flicking shakily
through the rule book again.

'Rule 32,' she announced. 'In accordance with the
powers invested in him/her, the secretary may at his/her
discretion impose a suspension or fine ...'

'You're suspending me?'

'Yes, and even if I say so myself, I believe I'm being more
than lenient.'

'But what have I done?'

'You know very well what you've done. You have
behaved abominably. You are a disgrace to the good name
of this club,' Mrs Mackey went on and every repetition of
the word 'you' came with disgusted emphasis: 'You are
over aggressive, loud-mouthed and every member of this

club is sick to death of putting up with YOU!'

Lida struggled to contain herself. She knew well that arguing with Mrs Mackey would only make things worse but she wasn't about to let this woman get the better of her.

'And I'm sick to death of putting up with you,' she said. 'Licking up to Ginny ... Miss Virginia Stannix, as if she was some kind of princess or something.'

Mrs Mackey sat back stony-faced on her chair. It was clear that with every word Lida was adding days to her suspension.

'Just because you hate me, you think everyone else does too,' she snarled. 'Show me one complaint you got about me. No? You can't because you're just making it all up. And you're lying about the draw. I know you are.'

Even as she spoke, Lida was thinking of Mags. It wasn't true that the club secretary was the only one who despised her. And the others? All the others? Could it really be the case that she was disliked by absolutely everybody?

Mrs Mackey leaned forward, her lips puckered spitefully.

'Do you have any friends in this club?' she hissed, 'even one?'

Lida stepped back as if she'd taken a blow to the stomach. There was no answer to the cruel question.

'I thought not,' said Mrs Mackey, taking command of the brittle silence in the small stuffy room. 'Did you ever stop to think why? And I was the one who nominated you as a member of this club as a favour to your mother. I should have had more sense.'

In the face of these awful truths there was no escape for Lida. Her legs refused to move and it was as if her body was insisting that she stay here and listen, no matter how painful it might be.

'We don't mind when someone gets upset with themselves in the heat of a game. It's only natural. But with you it's different. You have to take it out on your opponent. The fact is you intimidate people. At heart, you see, you're a bully.'

Coming from Mrs Mackey this last accusation was quite laughable. But Lida wasn't smiling. She was deathly pale and beginning to feel decidedly faint. Mrs Mackey could see this clearly. However, she had no sympathy for Lida. Now that she'd begun to say the things she'd bottled up since last year's final she was determined to go all the way.

'Then again, and I'm not saying this out of any disrespect for your hard-working parents, but your behaviour is hardly surprising given that you're a ... well, a foreigner,' she said. 'If it wasn't for men like Ginny's father sacrificing their lives you people might have bullied all of us into concentration camps and ...'

'I'm not German,' Lida shouted. 'You stupid woman, you understand nothing. My father lost everything he had because of Hitler.'

There was no point in going on. The explanation, even if she could state it clearly, would be lost on Mrs Mackey. Her sickly grin was evidence enough that she would only believe what she wanted to believe.

'How long am I suspended for?'

'It was my original intention,' Mrs Mackey enunciated, 'to suspend you for one day, but given your despicable attitude I've decided to extend it to three days.'

Having half-expected to be suspended for the entire championship, Lida felt quite relieved but couldn't resist a parting shot as she stepped out into the corridor.

'It doesn't matter,' she said, 'it'll probably be raining anyway.'

She closed the door in mock politeness and went through the shade-filled pavilion into the daylight again. The boys on the main court were making their usual ham-fisted attempts to look like real tennis players.

The scrawny one with his greasy brown hair guffawed loudly.

'Lida, you have two chances of beating Ginny Stannix,' he sneered; 'slim and none.'

His pal, a tall red-haired boy, face crimson from his exertions, joined in the laughter. Without breaking stride or bothering to look in their direction, Lida soon silenced them.

'Did anyone ever tell you,' she said, 'you're supposed to hit the ball over the net, not into it? You should try it some time. You mightn't look like such a pair of chimpanzees if you did.'

She was already in the lane beyond the court before either of them had stumbled on a reply. When the greasy-haired fellow called after her she had to smile, he sounded such a clown.

'Hey, watch it!' he yelled, 'or I'll … I'll tell Mrs Mackey on you.'

By the time she'd reached the gate at the end of the lane her smile had dissolved. The smart and often cruel answers that came so naturally to her always gave her an intensely spiteful pleasure when she spat them out. However, this pleasure invariably gave way to a sickening self-hate. Sometimes, as now, it seemed to her that there were two Lidas. One was quiet and reasonable. The other, loud and vindictive. She had no doubt what lay at the root of this second, hateful side. Her Germanness.

She dawdled through the town looking at nothing in particular in the shop windows. The square was maddeningly quiet as it always was, except on fair days when it was full of farm animals being bought and sold and the high-spirited banter of farmers and cattle dealers echoed across the open spaces.

The huge silence of the place left her feeling more alone than ever. The friendly nods of the very few passersby

served only to make her more aware of her own friendlessness. She looked at the sky hoping to see it darken. She'd
waited so long for the sun and now all she wanted was
rain. In the distance, there were indeed some clouds but
they seemed too white and wispy to offer any promise of
a deluge.

In five days the first round of the championship would
begin. That left two days for her to practise. She drew some
comfort from the fact that her opponent, Josie Hayes,
wasn't a real threat to her. Trying not to be too unkind, she
remembered the weaknesses of the girl's game and felt
reassured. The only problem she was likely to have was
with her shabby racket.

She thought of her father poring over his photograph,
so bound up in his own despair that small concerns such
as tennis rackets meant nothing to him. She remembered
his fury, his German fury, when any of them intruded on
his silent vigil. Though he'd never struck out at any of
them, his words could cause more pain than a blow.

'*Du dummes Kind!*'

She was no stupid child, she objected, as the mean
terraced houses of Garravicleheen came into view. Knowing it would cause her only more misery, she took a detour
just beyond the railway bridge to the site of the new
factory houses. Here, the air was alive with the hammer-
ing and laughter of workmen busily completing the large
semi-detached houses which her father refused to make
up his mind about.

It was time to make a real protest, she knew. They
couldn't go on like this any more. The uncertainty of it all
was too much for any family to bear without falling apart
at the seams. But what could she do? He wouldn't listen
to anything she said, no more than he would listen to her
mother or to Tommy.

Then it dawned on her and it seemed the sky, for a brief

instant, became infinitely brighter than it already was. She would refuse to speak German in the house from this moment on. She would shake her father from his selfish pining and if she persisted he would soon come to know that they'd all had enough of living in a lost world.

CHAPTER 5

These days, it was always easy to know whether Lida's father had come home for his dinner or stayed at the factory for some reason or other. She could tell by the sound of music or the absence of it. When he wasn't around the radio would be blaring in the kitchen or Tommy would be in his room playing his piano accordion. Sometimes, like today, it was both.

Somehow, it didn't seem fair to Lida to begin her protest before her father returned. Her mother was, after all, just as much a victim of the situation as she herself. Lida knew too that her mother had a way of getting around her and might convince her not to go ahead with her plan. She decided that it would be better to avoid the kitchen altogether and she went directly to her room.

Her father wouldn't be back for at least four hours but she was determined to wait. As she lay on her bed listening to the lively strains of the accordion she felt a terrible emptiness that no music could fill, felt invisible, felt almost that she might as well not have existed at all.

'Lida.' Her mother's call, quiet but insistent, snapped her to an unwelcome alertness. '*Das Mittagessen ist fertig.*'

The words, for all their ordinariness, grated on Lida's ears. 'Your dinner's ready.' She imagined some sinister SS officer barking out the phrase at Auschwitz or Teresensdat and saw the gaunt faces of the concentration camp prisoners glad to receive the smallest morsel from their gaolers. She couldn't bring herself to answer.

'Lida.'

The kitchen door closed below and the music in the next room stopped. Lida hoped that her mother was thinking she'd only imagined her daughter had come home. Shutting her eyes tight against the sun, Lida curled up and made herself small on the bed. She wasn't ready to face her mother, especially after making of her something she could never be – a monster. The door opened but she didn't look up.

'Why didn't you answer?'

At first, she was relieved to hear Tommy's voice. Then she remembered the freedom he was beginning to enjoy at their expense.

'I'm tired,' she said. 'Just leave me alone.'

'Hey,' he asked, coming closer, 'what's up, kid? It's not like you to miss your dinner.'

'I'm not hungry.'

He sat on the window-ledge by her bed and waited for her to open her eyes. She felt his gaze on her hunched-up form and drew her arms tighter still about herself.

'Stop looking at me.'

'Excuse me for living,' he laughed. 'You're tired and you're not hungry. Sounds serious. You're not in love, by any chance?'

'Don't you dare make fun of me.'

He raised the palms of his hands defensively but his wide grin was still in place.

'I was only trying to …'

'Just because I'm only fourteen, everyone thinks I can't have real … real problems. I'm supposed to be thick, am I? I'm supposed to have nothing between my ears only fresh air, that's what you think, isn't it? And Papa too!'

It was nothing new to him to hear Lida explode like this.

This time, however, there was an edge of anguish in her voice that caused him to show real concern.

'Something happened this morning, didn't it?'

'This morning!' she cried. 'Something's happening here every day. Can't you see that? Or are you too busy with your stupid music to notice that the rest of us are living in hell? In hell!'

'Lida,' he said soothingly, 'I know all that but there's something else. Why don't you tell me about it?'

She turned away from him and punched her pillow once, twice and kept punching until she could no longer keep count. Tommy reached across to her but she pushed his hand away.

'Don't touch me,' she said. 'I'm just a stupid child, like Papa says. You don't really want to know what happened. Nobody does.'

'Tell me, Lida.'

'It's not important. I just lost my only friend and got suspended from the tennis club for three days, that's all.'

'But you've often had rows with Mags before and ...'

'It was more than a row,' she insisted. 'She said awful things to me and I suppose I said worse.'

'And Mrs Mackey was picking on you again?' Tommy guessed. 'There's only one way to deal with her and that's by winning the championship again. And you will.'

'I will I'm sure. I've to play with a flippin' stick and Ginny Stannix has two new rackets.'

Tommy sat on the bed and she moved further away from him.

'Hey, I'm not going to touch you,' he said. 'I just want to tell you I invented even more reasons than you have before I went on stage but ...'

'I know, you realised after they were all just excuses and everything was hunky-dory on the night,' she sneered. 'Don't talk to me as if I was a child.'

'It would help if you didn't act like one.'

'Get out of my room, you home wrecker.'

Lida wasn't sure which she disliked most, when Tommy talked sense or when he teased. Right now it was all the same to her. Nothing could fill the aching chasm in the pit of her stomach, not even her anger with him.

'I don't even have one friend any more,' she said quietly.

'You have me.'

'You're my brother, that's not the same thing,' she said, and immediately cursed her insensitivity. 'I mean ...'

'I know what you mean,' Tommy told her. 'But, hey, that doesn't mean we can't stick together, right?'

'I suppose.'

'And you'll find another friend. People change their friends, you know. They kind of grow out of them, you know what I mean? I used to pal with Bobby Dunne but he was never interested in the same things I was, not after we got to fourteen or fifteen. That's how it goes. I still like Bobby but me and Johnny Tobin, well, we like the same music and films and all. We just have more to talk about.'

Pretending not to listen, Lida took in every word and tried to believe he was right. Somehow she knew that Tommy would always make friends more easily than she did. He wasn't as quick to fly off the handle, except with their father, and there was something calm about him, a calm she could never imagine in herself.

'We'd better go down,' he said finally. 'No point in upsetting Mama.'

Lida thought about telling him of her plan not to speak German but he too would certainly have tried to dissuade her. In any case, she had already decided that for the next few hours she would carry on as before. Even as she greeted her mother, the taste of German on her tongue didn't seem half so bad now that there was an end to it in sight.

The afternoon went by too slowly and there was too

much time to think and have doubts. Her mother seemed very pensive and spoke little. It was as though she sensed the coming storm. Lida hadn't told her about Mags or the trouble at the club, but it was clear she was aware of secrets behind Lida's erratic attempts to appear cheerful. Her mother didn't have to say anything. It was all in her face, a mixture of wisdom and tiredness, a troubled look that was all too frequent these past few months.

Minutes before her father was due to arrive home, Lida stood in the overgrown patch of garden watching the smoky-grey clouds she'd prayed for scudding by. She was startled by Tommy's voice and looked around in some confusion. He was upstairs, leaning out the back window.

'You're up to something,' he said.

'I am not,' she protested too eagerly.

'Yes, you are,' he insisted. 'I know by the look of you.'

He'd retreated before there was time to answer. She heard the creak of the front gate and the familiar tread of her father's hobnailed working boots on the pathway. If she stayed outside a moment longer she would lose the courage she'd built up so painstakingly all afternoon. She moved towards the back door of the kitchen.

Inside, Anna Hendel turned from the hot stove as her husband and daughter entered the kitchen at exactly the same moment, by different doors. Josef seemed unexpectedly bright and cheerful. This wasn't how Lida had pictured the scene earlier. She presumed he would be his usual sullen self. It would have been easier for her if he had been.

'*So ein schöner Sommertag*,' he said. '*Wie daheim, wie in Moravia.*'

Why couldn't he simply say it had been a beautiful day, Lida thought, without comparing it to 'home', to Moravia.

'I've been too busy working to notice,' Lida's mother said. She was glancing all the while at Lida who looked like she had something important to announce. Lida, however, had thought everything through in the inescapable argument, everything except her first words to him.

'I suppose you've been at the tennis club all day,' he chirped.

It occurred to her that instead of refusing to speak German she might refuse to speak at all until he came to his senses. But if she didn't speak, how would he know what her protest was about?

'I went to the club,' she said eventually, struggling unreasonably with the English language. 'But I could ... they would not ... couldn't play because they ... me ... suspended me.'

'Who suspended you?' he asked – in English.

So taken aback was Lida that she spoke without thinking. And her answer shocked and confused her even more.

'Frau Mackey,' she answered and then, too loudly, corrected herself: 'Missus Mackey.'

'Tomorrow when she comes,' her father said, returning to the language he was more comfortable with, 'I'll speak to her. I won't have this.'

'Please, Josef,' Anna interjected. 'It isn't worth fighting over. Maybe ... maybe we won't need to depend on her for much longer.'

He looked at her so coldly that Lida felt an icy tingling spread across the back of her neck. She was no longer concerned for herself but for her mother. He took his place at the kitchen table and picked up the knife lying alongside his plate. He considered its sharp serrated edge and his own reflection on the mock-silver blade. Finally, he set it down on the table's oilcloth.

'There's a time and place to speak about these things, Anna,' he said, 'and this is neither the time nor the place.'

It wasn't the time nor the place, Lida raged silently, because silly, feeble-minded Lida was here. Her confusion was swept away, her determination fired to the point of eruption.

'Why shouldn't you talk about it now?' she asked.

Only now did her father realise what she was about. His attention, however, appeared to remain fixed on his wife. Lida wanted to shout at him to look at her when she was speaking to him.

'Since when,' he asked Anna, 'do we speak English at home?'

Anna ignored his question and tried to change the subject.

'What did you do to be suspended?'

The harsh tone of her mother's voice, for all its guttural German frankness, rang false. Neither Lida nor her father were fooled by the pretence.

'Nothing,' Lida said, 'I did nothing wrong and I'm not doing anything wrong now. I'm just talking.'

'Your mother can't understand you,' he said. 'Her English isn't good.'

'Mama understands perfectly well, don't you, Mama?'

'Lida, I won't tell you again,' he shouted. 'Speak German. Show some consideration for your mother.'

'This has nothing to do with Mama, you know that.'

Anna stood at the kitchen range, a soup ladle poised in her trembling hand.

'Speak in German,' he insisted.

'But why? Please tell me why?'

'Speak in German or don't speak at all!'

The sound of the soup ladle crashing against the metal hob of the range silenced them.

'*Ich verstehe*,' Anna said and, as if to keep the balance of this temporary peace, added, 'I understand.'

Still defiant, in spite of the wave of shame that would not go away, Lida strode wilfully to the back door.

'I'll never speak another word of German in this house,'

she declared.

'Then you'd better keep your mouth shut, child,' her father told her. 'I won't be defied in my own home again.'

Lida grabbed the door handle with her left hand and raised her right arm in Nazi salute.

'Heil Hitler!' she cried and dashed outside, the sound of his chair scraping along the floor in her wake.

Lost in the wilderness of the garden, she realised there was nowhere to run. All she could do was wait for him to find her. But he didn't come. Instead, she heard his voice raised once again and Tommy's too. She wondered what the neighbours must think of them with their endless bickering and door-slamming.

'I don't care what any of you think,' Lida cried out foolishly, unheard and unnoticed by anyone but herself.

And then the rain came and she stood beneath it, battered but cooled by each heavy drop. She laughed out loud as she thought of Mrs Mackey and how her evil intentions were being washed down the drain by this glorious downpour. But she thought of Mags too as the rain streamed down her olive-skinned face. And Ginny, in her beautiful secluded house at the edge of town. She imagined her lying languidly on a velvety chaise longue reading the poems of W.B. Yeats, unconcerned by the foul weather, supremely confident in her own ability.

'I'll beat you, Ginny Stannix,' she told the world.

But the world couldn't hear her above the clamour of its tears.

CHAPTER 6

For the next three days, Lida had good reason to wonder how pleasant things might be if all her wishes came to pass so easily. Rain was what she had wished for and the heavens had provided it – in bucketfuls. So much so that by the third day she began to worry whether the ground would dry out in time for the first round.

Already, she'd given up hope of getting in any practice before the fateful day. The courts were likely to be so saturated that Mrs Mackey wouldn't allow anyone to step on them. Anyone except Ginny Stannix. There would be no problem about her playing there. Even if the main court was, by now, one great puddle, she would have let Ginny use it, believing as she did that the blonde girl was a goddess capable of walking on water.

At home, Lida's refusal to speak German was having such little effect that her resolve was already weakening. Her father never addressed her and ignored her when she spoke. Tommy avoided the issue altogether by not talking to her when her father was around. Lida regarded this as an unforgivable betrayal. When she confronted him about his cowardice, it became clear he was simply softening his father for yet another blow.

'You might have told me what you were going to do,' Tommy protested when she found him in his room and went on the attack.

'That's not the point,' she raged. 'You said we should stick together and now you won't even support me.'

'Together, yeah, but this was your idea and it's daft.'

'So you've thought of something better, have you?'

'No … but …'

'But what? You're thinking, is it? How long do we have to wait for your thick brain to work something out?'

He turned his attention embarrassedly back to the detective novel he was pretending to read. After music this was his favourite pastime, following the antics of American private detectives. Lida had sneaked a read of one once by a fellow called Hammet. In the end she gave up trying to make sense of the story. As far as she could see, Tommy only read them for the smart lines, the 'wisecracks', as he called them. They made him feel, she imagined, as rough and grainy as the paper they were printed on.

'I'm trying to read,' he told her. 'It's a Raymond Chandler. Johnny Tobin got it from his uncle in London.'

'No time to talk to your sister,' Lida said, 'but loads of it to waste on that rubbish and up in the band room. I've a good mind to tell Mama what you were doing when you were fibbing about going up to Johnny Tobin's house to study.'

'Ah, quit it, Lida,' Tommy pleaded. 'I worked hard. I made up for the time in the band room, you know that.'

'Why won't you do this with me?' she asked desperately. 'Why won't you stand up to him too?'

Tommy pushed aside his book and brushed his hand through his fair hair.

'The fact is,' he explained, 'the band is going down to Dungarvan to play on Saturday night. We'll be playing until three in the morning and God knows what time we'll get back. Papa will hit the roof when I tell him so I have to go easy on him until then. It's going to be bad enough as it is.'

Lida retreated in disgust from his room. They weren't

in this together. That was the problem in this house.
They weren't a family, only a bunch of selfish individuals
worried about themselves and their own wants. All except
her mother and she was too quiet, too patient and nobody
knew what she really wanted. Apart from a peaceful
home. But was that enough? What good was peace when
so much ill-feeling was merely hidden away, ready to seep
through at any and every moment?

The next morning arrived as darkly as those before. Even
the knowledge that her suspension was now lifted failed
to improve Lida's humour. There had been more rain
during the night and the lowering sky promised no
change. She saw no point in getting up and pulled the
blankets over her head to make an even greater darkness
of the gloom.

Hours later, how many hours she had no idea, she was
woken by her mother's singing voice, the whish of opened
curtains, the cool rush of air as her blanket was swept back
and, most startingly of all, the red shock of sunlight over
her clenched eyelids. At first, the sickly sense of guilt that
filled her seemed to arise from the shame of her laziness.
Then she remembered her dream.

She sat up, oblivious to her mother's busy chatter. She
had dreamt about Ginny Stannix. No! She had dreamt she
was Ginny Stannix. But she hadn't dreamt that she was
beautiful or lived in a perfect, large-roomed house or that
she had everything she desired. And there was no new
tennis racket in this dream, only a huge emptiness. An
emptiness left by the absence of her own dead father.

How could she ever forgive herself if he really did die,
if he met with some terrible accident at work? And wasn't
that within the bounds of possibility? Only last year hadn't
that poor man, Eamon Dorney, fallen into a vat of boiling
sugar at the factory and almost died from his horrific

burns? What if there was no time to say she was sorry, no time to tell him that she loved him – for all his faults?

'You look like you've seen a ghost,' her mother laughed, not knowing how close to the truth she was.

'Is Papa home for his lunch yet?'

'It's ten past two, Lida,' her mother said. 'He's already gone back. Did you want to talk to him?'

'No ... I mean ...'

She didn't want to disappoint her mother nor did she want to raise her hopes. Already her mind was working on excuses not to call a truce in the row with her father. What if she herself was the one who died? How could he forgive himself? A new tennis racket would surely be a very small thing to him then. And, she thought, just because I love him doesn't mean he can't be wrong.

A shadow stained the bright room and darkened her mother's face.

'Maybe later,' Lida said.

Her mother turned to the window waiting for the shadow to pass. Standing quite still, her breath distant and shallow, she seemed to Lida like some angel abandoned on this harsh earth, the sky her only reminder of a lost heaven. Then the yellowy-gold light returned and it was as if it was radiating from her mother, through the wisps of fine brown hair tied up in a loose bundle with the wooden clip from her far away home.

'You know, I've noticed the berries are out very early this year. I wonder if that's a good sign,' Anna said.

'A good sign for what?'

'Oh, I don't know,' her mother sighed vaguely. 'Why don't we go out and see if we can find some?'

There was nothing she wouldn't have done for her mother at that moment. The chance to return to the club, so anxiously awaited, seemed unimportant now. The unpleasantness of her dream was forgotten as she searched for her emerald green summer dress. It was the only dress her mother had ever bought in a shop for her. That was three years ago.

When at last she found it, she was filled again with the same excitement as on that day down in Dempsey's in the square. She buried her face in the fresh cotton and the smell brought back the whole scene. The long counter covered with the dresses she'd already tried, the shelves behind stacked with lace-collared blouses and tartan skirts, and the big cardboard boxes on the floor, just by the long mirror, stuffed with balls of wool of every conceivable shade.

The dress had been much too long that first day but her mother turned it up. It had been bought to last and last it did, her mother working it up expertly each year. In truth, she hadn't grown a lot in those few years and though Lida bemoaned the fact, she was happy enough to ignore it since it allowed her to fit for so long into her favourite dress.

She slipped the green cotton over her shoulders and tugged it down. And tugged again. And again. She'd outgrown her childhood dress. The problem was no longer with the hem. The whole thing was simply too tight a squeeze. As she struggled to get out of it she was more surprised than disappointed. Pulling on the dress she'd worn the day before she felt weighed down by its heavy woollen fabric.

When finally she arrived at the kitchen door, her surprise was still there to be seen. Her mother glanced up from her preparation for the berry hunt and looked at Lida quizzically.

'The green summer dress doesn't fit me any more.'

'I could've told you that,' her mother smiled. 'These last few months you've really shot up.'

'Out is more like it,' Lida complained. 'I'm fat.'

'Fat? You don't have an ounce to spare.'

Lida wasn't convinced. She felt gross and the day was spoiled for her. She imagined that if they did find any early berries along the country roads, they would be half-eaten away by worms or rotted away on their stems. She wondered if her mother was simply fooling herself into believing the berries were out. It was a time she had always seemed at her happiest, perhaps because it reminded her so much of her childhood in Moravia.

'Are you sure you actually saw the berries?' Lida asked, but her mother was too busy lining her two straw message bags with old newspapers to answer.

It felt all wrong to Lida: her mother's quiet, childlike insistence, and her own uncomfortable awareness of having grown so suddenly. It was almost as if they had swapped roles; her mother become a child and she herself an unwilling adult.

'Now then,' her mother declared, the task completed, 'we'll try the Cormackstown Road.'

Lida's sense of unease found, all at once, something very real to fasten itself on. The Cormackstown Road was where the Stannix family lived. It was the last place on earth she wanted to be.

'I hate that road,' she protested. 'The smell of old Carey's piggery is awful out there.'

'It's the best road for blackberries I know,' her mother said, 'and the smells of nature never killed anyone yet.'

'There's always a first time.'

'Cheer up, Lida,' her mother suggested as she handed over one of the carrier bags. 'There's plenty more of those dresses in Dempsey's.'

'I'm getting a new one?'

'Don't ask me to make promises now. We'll see.'

As they walked out beyond the huddled ranks of houses

in Garravicleheen to the open countryside, Lida felt far
from optimistic about ever getting a new dress or anything
else that could instead be made or bought second-hand. In
any event, dresses weren't important to her now.

'If you do buy me something,' she told her mother, 'I'd
prefer a tennis racket. I *need* a tennis racket.'

The still air was filled with sounds carried from great
distances. Laughing children, hammered echoes, low-
ing cattle. Her mother's thoughts were far away too. It
seemed a pity to disturb her from her trance, but Lida's
pity was reserved mainly for herself.

'My racket is falling apart.'

'We can't always have what we want.'

'But Papa has the money,' Lida replied. 'I could have a
new racket if he wasn't so stingy.'

Among the hedgerows, Anna spotted with a gasp of
delight and relief a bush rich with bunches of blackberries.
She began to gather them as if she'd already forgotten their
conversation. Lida stood behind her, growing more impatient as each berry was checked before being carefully
placed in the straw basket.

All this work, she thought angrily, for a few miserable
pots of jam and a few bottles of wine. The tangy sweet
smell of the kitchen as her mother prepared these things,
an aroma that gave Lida goosepimples it was so beautiful,
seemed too meagre a prize for the drudgery it involved.

'It's ten years since he lost the farm,' Lida cried. 'Why
can't he just forget about it?'

Her mother seemed to consider the question with far
less concentration than she was putting into examining
the purple flesh of the berries. It was almost a surprise
when she did finally answer, so remote was the look in her
eyes.

'Ten years, yes, ten years should be a long time,' she
said, 'but time is a strange thing. My grandmother,

Marthe, you remember all those stories I told you about her? Such a funny woman, so full of life, right up to the end. When she was eighty-five, it must have been, she was still dancing like a girl. The polka: you should have seen her dance a polka.'

The deep wine blush stained her fingers now and a soft pink glow entered her cheeks. Her whole body shook with chuckling.

'Whenever there was a dance in the village hall she'd spend hours getting ready. Then she'd have all of us there waiting for the doors to open. The really funny thing was that if the best-looking boys in the village didn't dance with her she'd be so disappointed. When she danced, you see, she thought she was young and beautiful again. Time meant nothing to her.'

Lida wasn't quite sure where this was leading. To her it was just another story, another memory, another step back into a vanished past.

'You see, Lida, there are two kinds of time. One of them is ticking away there on the clock, second after second, minute after minute. It never stops racing on. But the other time is kept inside, in people's minds. A time that is different for everybody, and has nothing to do with the ticking clock. My grandmother could imagine it was only yesteday that she was seventeen. Your father is the same. Yes, ten years sounds like a long time but for him it's as if that terrible tragedy has just happened. It's so close to his heart, you see, that time doesn't come into it. Not real time.'

If it was true that time passed more slowly for her great-grandmother and for her father, then it was equally true that for Lida time was rushing too quickly. The day of the first round of the championship was almost upon her and she was completely unprepared. Even this afternoon, hours were being wasted. In her mind the two days remaining were already passed and she was on court being beaten by Josie Hayes, a girl who should have had no chance against her.

The blackberry bush had yielded most of its fruits to Anna and they moved on. Turning right at the top of the road leading from town they headed towards Cormackstown. In the distance the ring of trees surrounding the Stannix estate came into view. Lida's stomach tightened and a bitter taste filled her mouth. She dipped a hand into her mother's bag and drew out a berry. It was sweet and luscious as it burst on her tongue but a grainy seed lodged uncomfortably between her teeth and wouldn't come loose.

Beneath the shadow of the six-foot high wall of the estate, Lida went ahead of her mother, trying to hurry by. As she neared the white, freshly-painted front gate overhung on both sides by giant oaks, some familiar sounds assailed her ears. The thwack and pop of a tennis ball being struck, the rush of feet, softly pounding the grassy earth, and Mags Campion's shrill cry of exasperation.

She looked disbelievingly in along the winding lane leading to the large red-bricked house with its white timber arches over the windows. Trees and shrubbery obscured her view but between the branches she caught a glimpse of the tennis court laid out on the front lawn. Then she saw Ginny Stannix and Mags pause in their game and begin to talk animatedly. Lida couldn't avoid the feeling that she was the subject of their conversation. The empty bag was heavy in her hand and too large to hide as she wanted so desperately to do.

Then, adding to her embarrassment, Ginny waved to her and called out something Lida couldn't hear. Mags turned the other way and appeared to be laughing. Lida swung around and to her horror saw that her mother was waving back at Ginny.

'What are you doing?' Lida exclaimed. 'You don't even know her.'

'Isn't that other girl your friend Mags?'

'No.'

'I'm sure it is, Lida. Why don't you go and talk to her? I can collect the berries. I've probably found the best of them anyway.'

'No,' Lida insisted and stalked away, swinging her bag as if at any moment she might fling it over the stone wall and in among the trees that kept guard on this oasis of comfortable splendour.

Ten yards ahead of her mother now, she surrendered her whole being to the struggle to remove the blackberry seed from between her teeth. She poked at it vengefully with the tip of her tongue. She wanted to be rid of it as badly as she wanted to be rid of the memory of Ginny and Mags sneering at her.

Nearing the end of the estate wall she began to be aware of a peculiarly high-pitched humming. At first, it almost seemed like the noise was coming from somewhere inside her. Then she realised that it came from among the vast thicket of leaves above her head. It sounded like no bird she'd ever heard before nor any small animal, for that matter. She stopped as the sound revealed itself as unmistakably human.

Her mother had drawn close to her side and she too was peering into the branches above, curiously. Lida saw him first. She grabbed her mother's arm.

It was Hubert Stannix, Ginny's uncle, with his electric shock of grey hair atop a boyish face. He swayed sadly and, softly, his voice was singing. A lullaby, the gentle sound of a child coaxing an infant to sleep. Only two words reached Lida and her mother's ears, repeating themselves over and over.

'Swing-ing tree. Swing-ing tree.'

The rest was lost in the faint rustle of leaves.

'Don't stare,' her mother whispered and tugged Lida away. 'We'll come back by the Beakstown Road.'

If Lida needed something to distract her from her own troubles, Hubert Stannix had provided it. The whole town said he was quite mad but he didn't inspire fear in Lida. What she felt was pity and this in itself was surprising. She'd never imagined she'd ever feel sorry for a Stannix.

Now she wondered how perfect that home really was with its manicured gardens and its rustic, red-bricked beauty. Surely Hubert's madness, for all its seeming gentleness, seeped into every pore of that once magical place. And into the hearts of those who lived there.

CHAPTER 7

The Junior Championship began on a day that was dull in every sense of the word. The sky formed a colourless backdrop to Lida's and Josie Hayes's indifferent efforts in a match that stuttered from one blunder to the next. Lida won only because Josie's blunders were more spectacular and regular than her own. At the pavilion steps a few disinterested stragglers watched the two girls as if they were two insignificant flies wandering inexpertly up a wall.

Lida's lack of match practice showed all too clearly but there were other reasons for her poor performance. Her unwelcome burst of growth, the echo of Ginny and Mags's laughter and the unsettling recollection of Hubert Stannix in his high perch heaped further confusion on her already troubled state of mind. The victory over Josie Hayes didn't help. Somehow she knew it was of little consequence. It was like winning a skirmish when, all the while, you were losing the war.

Her protest at home had all but fizzled out. Only her mother had been hurt by it and she was the last one Lida wanted to hurt. She hadn't spoken to her father yet but knew she soon would. Her willpower was as weak and useless as the racket which had, once more, let her down in today's match.

She offered her hand to Josie and received in return a

cold-fish handshake.

'I had to let you win,' Josie said, famous for her excuses. 'I'm going to Tullamore tomorrow to my aunt and I won't be back for two weeks.'

After a match, Lida would normally be so keyed up that she'd never let a remark like this pass. Today she couldn't be bothered.

'Have a nice time,' she said but Josie had already turned her back on her.

Lida trudged across to the pavilion and inside, her steps seemed to fall more heavily than those of all the others on the timber floor. She felt miserably self-conscious in the dressing-room as the more well-off girls decked themselves out in their starched whites.

Her own pleated white skirt just about fitted her now but the blouse she kept specially for tennis was as uncomfortably tight as the green dress had been. It had kept her from stretching to several shots during the match with Josie and, even more than her racket, this had made her seem a less than average player. The furtive glances of those around her seemed to be asking the same question: how could she possibly have become Junior Champion?

The panic she felt at the sound of Mags's voice from the Pit, behind the pavilion, was overwhelming. She picked up her towel and racket quickly and made for the front door. It was too ridiculous but she didn't want to meet Mags, didn't want Mags to see her. As she rushed down the steps into the grey afternoon, Josie Hayes was turning the corner of the pavilion.

'Mags is winning,' she announced with a supercilious grin.

Mags had never won a match in her life and the girl she was facing, Maeve Reilly, had reached the quarter-finals last year. Lida thought she'd sneak a look, thinking that Josie was just trying to be smart. It wouldn't have been the first time she'd made fun of Mags. As she approached the Pit, Lida knew again that protective feeling she'd often had towards her former friend. That urge to defend Mags from the cruel jibes of other girls. It was a feeling complicated now by the fact that Lida had, in her own way, joined the ranks of these insult-bearers.

To her surprise, Lida found that Josie had, for once, been telling the truth. Though struggling a little now, Mags was giving as good as she got against her more athletic opponent. Lida became totally absorbed in the match, willing Mags to win, in spite of everything.

So embarrassed had Maeve become at being matched at every turn by the big girl that she began to lose her touch entirely. In the end, Mags won to a round of astonished applause and no one clapped louder than Lida. Sweat poured from Mags's unhealthily mottled face as Lida went to congratulate her. Her hand was wet, the pudgy fingers more swollen than ever when Lida pumped it enthusiastically.

'I said you were good,' Lida declared, knowing at once that she never had.

Mags was too excited by her win to notice Lida's guilty discomfort.

'It was Ginny,' she said. 'She made me believe I could do it.'

Lida's hand fell limply from Mags's loosened grip.

'She's so patient, so kind ...'

Pushed aside by the other well-wishers, Lida stood at the edge of the small crowd wondering why she couldn't just withdraw and spare herself further humiliation. Soon she found herself standing face to face with Mags, knowing she wanted to say something, not knowing what to say. Mags brushed by her and went towards the pavilion.

'Mags,' Lida called, swallowing her pride, 'I'll come up to your house some day. Tomorrow, maybe.'

Mags appeared to hesitate but went on. Suddenly she wheeled around with a look made to wound.

'Why did you never ask me up to your house?' she asked.

'You know how small and … miserable it is,' Lida stuttered. 'It's not like your home, all …'

'Frilly?' Mags said coldly.

'I didn't mean to say that.'

'But you did say it. Anyway, you're only making excuses. There's something you want to hide, isn't there?'

It was as though all the heartache and misery of the house in Garravicleheen had been exposed for everyone to see. How could Mags have known about all that? How, when she'd never even listened to Lida's wasted attempts to explain where her family had come from, and why they were stranded like survivors from a shipwreck?

'I have nothing to hide,' she said.

'I know why you didn't want me in your house and it's not because it's so small, it's something else.'

'What goes on in my house is none of your business.'

'Well, I know what you're hiding,' Mags said and added mysteriously, 'and I know someone who saw it.'

'Saw what?'

'With their own eyes, Lida Hendel. And I believe them!' Mags shouted and disappeared around the side of the pavilion leaving Lida alone in the Pit.

What was Mags raving about? What was it that 'someone' had seen? Surely not the endless arguments, not the miserliness of her father, not the dark spell they all lived under? No, she seemed to be talking about some specific thing, some object. But what?

She thought about charging into the pavilion and demanding to know what was on Mags's mind. But the greyness, the sheer turgid weight of the sky above, broke her will. Gathering the little strength she had left, she walked by the humming pavilion and the empty main court to the grassy lane without a backward glance. She didn't care if she never saw the place again.

This time she took no detour to the new factory houses or anywhere else as she wandered wearily home. Her muscles ached and she wished there was a nice welcoming bath to fall into in her house, like the one in Mags's. But in Garravicleheen there was only the kitchen sink or the tub, to be filled with kettles of boiling water from the stove. Having a bath now would be more trouble than it was worth.

The quietness of the house, when she went inside, was almost eerie. Her mother wasn't in and had, she guessed, gone down town for the messages. Today was her father's pay-day, the day the 'big shopping', as her mother described it, was done in Johnston's on the square. The 'big shopping' consisted of filling the two small straw bags with those few things that couldn't be made at home – tea, flour, bicarbonate of soda, dried fruit. There were few 'small shoppings' and never even one packet of Fig Rolls or Ginger Nut or plain Marietta biscuits.

As her mother set out each Thursday afternoon she would be as nervous as if it were her first outing in a strange town. After all the years she knew hardly a soul in the place and her poor grasp of English ensured it would remain so. She was regarded as unfriendly but was, in fact, simply shy and confused. Lida knew it helped when she went along and that she should go to meet her now, but she wanted only to hide from the town and all its people.

She set about making herself a cup of tea and had only just turned the tap when she realised she wasn't alone in the house. From Tommy's room came the familiar squeak of the wardrobe door opening and closing several times. She thought to go and tell him about her match. He was always enthusiastic about her tennis-playing and maybe he'd raise her spirits and help her feel some satisfaction after her victory.

Mounting the stairs she began to wonder what all the shuffling around up there was about. It almost sounded like a scuffle except there were no raised voices. She knocked at his door, as he always insisted she should. When he didn't answer she eased open the door and peered inside.

On the bed lay a suitcase she'd never seen before, its gaping mouth receiving untidy bundles of shirts and trousers flung from the wardrobe. Tommy, on his knees, looked up from his search of the bottom drawer.

'Is my blue shirt in the wash?' he asked offhandedly.

'I don't know, why don't you ask the maid?'

She didn't need to ask what was happening. Tommy, she knew, was leaving as he'd often threatened to do of late. While Lida had never quite taken the threat seriously she wasn't surprised now to see it come to pass.

'Why are you going?' she asked. 'I mean, why now?'

'I just had a barney with the old man,' Tommy answered, taking false courage from the glib words of his detective heroes.

'You two are always at it. What's different this time?'

Tommy got to his feet with a stack of bundled socks and as he spoke he used the suitcase for target practice. He kept missing.

'He's throwing me out is what's different.'

'You told him you were going to Dungarvan with the band, I suppose.'

'Yeah. And he said if I went I wasn't to come back. Ever.' He hit the target with a pair of red socks, the ones that so annoyed his father.

Hardly aware of what she was doing, Lida moved around picking up the socks from the floor. She always refused point-blank to tidy up after her brother. But this didn't feel like tidying up. It felt more like a desperate attempt to keep things together, to stop the spreading chaos that had invaded her family.

'Where will you stay? Johnny Tobin's?'

He turned to the wardrobe and fingered the remaining clothes as if to choose between them. Lida wasn't fooled by the pretence.

'Where are you going to stay?'

'Ger Kinsella's,' he muttered.

His broad back made an ideal target for Lida. She wished she had something more substantial to throw at him other than this revolting pair of canary yellow socks. It was bad enough that he was leaving, but to go and live with that miserable drunkard, Kinsella – that was too much. At last, she found something to hit him with.

'How could you do this to Mama?' she asked.

'There's no room in Johnny's,' he answered weakly, 'not since the uncle came back from England.'

Lida pelted the yellow socks at him without conviction. Her aim was slightly off and the small bundle hit the wardrobe door. It swayed slowly back and in the long inner mirror she saw his face. His eyes were moist and his chin sagged tremulously.

'The big tough man,' she said, feeling the utter futility of her name-calling. 'Mister Tommy Hendel, private investigator.'

'Cripes, Lida, give it a rest, will you.'

'Hard-chaw Hendel.'

'I know I'm not,' he said. 'I'd be better off if I didn't care about anybody or anything.'

'Don't make me sick,' she breathed and stumbled to the door, kicking the mess of clothes out of her way.

Their eyes met in the mirror-distance.

'Come up and see me some time.'

'I will I'm sure,' she spat out. 'One rat hole is enough for me to bear.'

In her own room she waited for her mother to return, thinking it wasn't too late to stop this madness. Angry talk was one thing, but now that it had come to this – the first real fracture of her family – the outcome had a frightening inevitability about it. The beginning of the end for all of them loomed. Only her mother could hold them together.

Lida was out of her room and down the stairs before Anna had reached the kitchen door.

'Tommy's packing his bags up there.'

'I know,' Anna said and left Lida standing in the hallway, the last shreds of hope sundered by this unexpectedly calm reaction.

'You know?' Lida inquired, alone in the narrow space between the stained and weeping walls.

From the kitchen her mother's words came with a quiet force.

'We've talked about it,' she said, 'and Tommy's made his choice.'

Lida felt the chill of damp spread through her. Her very bones seemed to bend with it as she walked into the dark kitchen.

'How can you let Papa do this?'

'Tommy made up his own mind.'

'He was thrown out like a dog!'

Her mother was putting away the messages one by one on to the top shelf of the cupboard she'd painted only yesterday, inside and out. Once a month she went meticulously about this task of covering up the dank, malignant rain of dampness. The colour varied according to what Josef could get from the leftover paint tins up at the factory store. Right now it was an off-puttingly streaky mixture of brown and green.

On the bottom shelf was the only thing there was plenty of in this house. Sugar; damp, lumpy sugar in half-pound paper bags. As a child Lida would eat sugar by the fistful if left alone in the kitchen for more than a minute. Now the thought of that gritty sweetness sickened her. She could remember the very day, a few months back, when her stomach turned against it. Not from any gluttonous over-indulgence but from her father's sour words.

The dark mood had been over him for weeks, over all of them. He rarely spoke and never at such length as on that evening. Their silent meal had reached the rare treat of dessert. An apple tart, sprinkled gener-ously on its top with sugar, the lumps teased out to a white sand of crystals. Lida and Tommy devoured it. Their mother ate slowly as always, savouring every morsel as if to prove to herself that all the trouble she took in the making of it, and in every other chore besides, was worthwhile. Josef Hendel stared at the tart on his plate as though it were the work of some devil.

'There's too much sugar on this,' he complained.

'Just scrape it off then,' his wife replied, still lost in her slow delight.

'So much sugar, all you can taste is sugar. Does it taste too sweet to you?' he asked of Tommy.

'No.'

'Lida?'

'No, Papa.'

'You like the taste of sugar, do you?'

'Please, Josef,' her mother pleaded.

'What does it taste of?' he wanted to know.

'It's just ... sweet,' Tommy answered dourly.

'You think so? Try some more. Now, can you taste something else? Can you taste the sweat of the farmer in his field of sugar beet? The lorry driver's sweat? The men at the unloading bay? And the sugar-cook's sweat? My sweat? And the little bits of our souls, the huge chunks of our wasted lives? Can you taste them?'

He pushed back his chair and went to his room. To his faded photograph. After this incident, Tommy ate more sugar than ever but Lida couldn't so much as look at a sealed bag of it without feeling ill.

'Mama,' she asked as her mother closed the cupboard door, 'where is it going to end?'

Her mother looked over her shoulder. Tommy was at the kitchen door.

'See you when I see you, folks,' he said, eking out a brave smile from his devastated face.

'Be good,' his mother said and moved towards him.

He backed away into the hallway and they heard him rush to the front door and out by the creaky gate. Lida made to follow him but her mother held her back. She shook her head and was about to speak but changed her mind. Lida's words barely stirred the silence.

'I wish it was Papa who was gone,' she said.

She thought of Ginny, the girl without a father. She doesn't know how lucky she is, Lida told herself.

'I do. I wish he'd just go away.'

CHAPTER 8

As Lida entered her brother's room next morning she knocked on the door from sheer force of habit. She felt foolish as she stared at the empty bed, stripped down to the bare, patched mattress. Her mother never let the work wait. Lida looked out into the garden and saw the linen sheets flapping on the clothesline. It seemed her mother, no less than her father, had washed her hands of Tommy.

For a moment she imagined that they were her own bedclothes. Would they accept her going as easily as they appeared to accept Tommy's? But the thought was absurd. She was only fourteen. Even if she did leave, where could she go? No matter where she went, the guards would have her back home within the hour.

Then, an even more absurd notion took root in her mind. Or was it so absurd? If she went and stayed with Tommy, even for a little while, wouldn't that shake her father from his obstinate ways more than her present silence was ever likely to? People said that Ger Kinsella's house was in a dreadful state but she could tackle it. She had plenty of practice here in Garravicleheen.

Furthermore, the talk about Ger's drinking habits were, as far as she was concerned, merely rumour. She'd never *seen* him drunk. So busy was she convincing herself, it didn't occur to her that she was never on the streets after pub closing time.

The only regret would be in having to leave her mother, but surely they would sort out the whole mess between them once they realised how far things had gone?

An old street rhyme came singing itself into her mind. 'Ten Green Bottles'. Except that, in this case, it was 'Four Green Bottles'.

'Four green bottles standing on a wall.
Four green bottles standing on a wall.
And if one green bottle should accidentally fall,
There'd be three green bottles standing on a wall.
Three green bottles standing on a wall ...'

The lilt of the rhyme made Lida sad. It was no longer the happy tune of her childhood games but the sombre overture to an impossible decision. In the end she decided, as people often do, to put off the fateful choice. She would go to meet Tommy, have a good look around the house and maybe then she'd be better able to decide whether or not to stay with him.

Kickham Street was at the far end of town. She had no idea which house was Ger's but guessed it would stand out from all the others. However, when she got there, she had to ask an old woman leaning out over a half-door at the end of nearby Church Lane.

'Up along there on the left. The one with the blue door,' the woman said, throwing her eyes up to heaven. 'Hold on, no. It's the second one with a blue door. Maisie Kelly painted hers the other day. I'd swear they fecked the paint. Them Kellys, they're a right bunch of ...'

The woman was still talking when Lida reached Ger's two-storey terraced house. The colour was only a dusty memory of blue by now. Lida peered in by the front window, her persistent knocking ignored though there was certainly someone moving about inside.

'He don't get up till the sun come down,' the woman cackled in the distance.

Tapping at the window, Lida saw a shape pass by a door at the far side of the front room. She heard footsteps in the hallway and pushed in the letter box to see if it was Tommy. Before her was the shocking spectacle of Ger Kinsella, his big belly protruding from an open pyjama top. The folds of fat on his chin sagged unshaven, and a fuzzy ball of hair atop his otherwise bald head stood up in wild disarray. He padded to the door and opened it just enough to see who was there.

'Jaysus,' he said, relieved. 'I thought it was the rent man. Come in, girl.'

Lida hesitated at the threshold but he'd already turned and was shuffling away to the back of the house.

'He's above in the boxroom,' he called over his shoulder. 'Top of the landing. Straight in front of you. Tell him I'm making tea.'

She waited until he was out of sight, slammed the door and bolted up the stairs. The carpet stuck to the soles of her shoes with every step. She burst in on Tommy and found him buried beneath a pile of soiled blankets. The room smelled of stale cigarettes, the bare floorboards were streaked with the silvery trails of snails and peppered with bits of dry clay. There was no wardrobe or dresser. Tommy's borrowed suitcase lay dejectedly in a corner, yesterday's clothes in a heap on its musty top.

'Tommy,' Lida said, 'it's all hours in the day, would you ever get up.'

Her brother emerged looking tired and sick. He had trouble keeping his eyes open and he clutched his fair head in his hands. When he saw it was Lida he covered his face with the blankets.

'You have a hangover,' she muttered in disgust.

'No, I don't,' he said, his voice muffled by the spittle-stained pillow.

'You look worse than that fellow down below.'

Tommy sat up and drew his hands away from his head, trusting it to stay in place and not topple off, as he seemed to expect it to.

'Such a night,' he moaned.

'I can just imagine.'

'It's not like you think,' he said, screwing up his eyes towards the window. 'First of all, I smoked twenty fags before I went on I was so nervous. Then I got sick in the car coming home and I swear I wasn't drinking.'

Lida glowered disdainfully around the hideous bedroom. She could never live in a place like this, no matter what the circumstances.

'Is this what you call "freedom"?' she asked.

'It's not as bad as it looks.'

'No, it's worse,' she said. 'It's a kip. I was actually feeling sorry for you, Tommy. But anyone who could let themselves live like this doesn't deserve sympathy.'

The effort of sitting up had become too much for Tommy. He lay back and closed his eyes.

'Look, Lida,' he said, 'I won't be stopping here long. I'm going to Dublin in a few weeks to try out for a Big Band. Some pal of Ger's who's doing really well. Ger says it'd be a great break for me.'

There was nothing to sit on but the filthy bed so she remained standing. If Tommy stayed in town, she and her mother would at least see him occasionally. The thought of him far away in Dublin left her feeling desperately lonely.

'When I get a bit of experience up there,' he said, brightening up, 'I'm heading for London. You'd never know, I might end up in the Jack Hylton Orchestra. You might even hear me on the radio.'

'Yeah,' Lida said. 'I could have a great chat with you on the radio. Why don't you go to America while you're at it? You might meet some of those stupid detectives you're always reading about.'

'I might just do that,' Tommy answered, lifting his head from the pillow again. 'See, you can do anything you want if you believe in yourself and aren't afraid to take the first step.'

Some first step, she thought, from a hovel to a hole in the ground.

'You'll get your chance too. Some day. But in the meantime you have to keep your mind on the tennis and forget all the rest.'

'Tennis isn't important any more,' she said bitterly.

''Course it is. You're good at it. It's your way of getting through the nonsense at home. I have my piano playing, you have tennis, Papa has his dumb photograph, Mama has ...'

Either words failed him or he couldn't face the truth. One way or the other he couldn't say any more. Lida, however, thought she knew what it was her mother had and she wasn't about to let Tommy off the hook so easily.

'Us?' she asked.

'Maybe so.'

'Then why did you leave?'

'Open the window, would you?' Tommy pleaded, only now aware of the fetid stench of the room.

Lida too had had enough of the evil-smelling atmosphere. She stepped cautiously across the grimy floor to the door.

'Open it yourself,' she told him.

'Lida, I'm sorry it's such a mess but as soon as I get a few bob together I'll be out of here.'

'You'll end up like Kinsella.'

Tommy's look contained such certainty and determination that she could almost believe in him again as he spoke.

'Never,' he said. 'Ger is in a rut. Things just went wrong for him and he gave up. I'll never let that happen to me. Never.'

She left him staring at the empty doorway, walked with Mrs Mackey-like steps down the tacky stairs and closed out the front door with a farewell bang. She couldn't get out of Kickham Street quickly enough and pressed on towards the square.

The mere act of walking was a struggle, she felt so drained. No one listened to her – maybe they never had. The easiest thing to do was to stay quiet in the face of her tormentors. Her father, Mrs Mackey, Ginny and Mags, even Tommy. When the time came she could simply slink away from Garravicleheen, from this town, and never return.

Lida might well have followed this course as dispirit-edly as she followed the path through the square, if the word 'surrender' hadn't begun to repeat itself more vehe-mently with every onward step. She fought it, tried to erase it with other, more acceptable, words. 'Sensible'. 'Reasonable'. And other phrases. 'No other choice', 'what's the point?', 'a quiet life'. But there was no escape from the accusation of craven submission.

The window of Molloy's Hardware Store held no inter-est for Lida as she stood before it, unable to move on. It was her own reflection there which mesmerised her. A small, dark-haired girl with a steely-eyed grittiness that was far from the soft, malleable confusion of emotions Lida felt. A stranger, a 'foreigner'. Lida Hendel. She re-peated the name as if to convince herself that the strength portrayed in this girl's features was her own.

There could be no question of giving up, only one of deciding where the next pitched battle was to take place. The answer came from the reflected image of a tree-lined avenue leading off the other side of the square. The Mall. Where Mags Campion lived.

*

Mrs Campion answered the door frostily with folded arms and pursed lips.

'Could I speak to Mags, please?'

She half-closed the door and retreated silently into the frilly depths and after a long delay, Mags appeared, looking flustered and uneasy. Lida hadn't expected to be asked in, but left standing at the door she'd felt like a beggar; this made her less circumspect than she might have been. Now she was goaded into a directness that had Mags sweating, in spite of the cold breeze being sucked in by the open door.

'I want to know what it is someone's supposed to have seen in my house.'

'Your house?' Mags muttered, feigning bewilderment.

'Tell me!'

A trail of spittle began to emerge from the corner of Mags's wavering mouth. She wiped it on the sleeve of her dress. Her eyes were filled to brimming. One word, Lida knew, and she could have the big girl blubbering like a beached whale.

'I'm not blaming you, Mags,' she said. 'I know this is something somebody told you to say. I just want the truth.'

Mags didn't take too kindly to being pitied. She slid half in behind the door, using it as a shield.

'As if you didn't know,' she parried. 'Aren't you looking at it every day?'

'Looking at what?'

'The picture of Adolf Hitler on your mantelpiece in your kitchen. The one your father put up when the war was going your way.'

The accusation exploded into Lida's mind with such force that for a moment she couldn't remember whose photograph actually hung there. She could almost believe that what Mags said was true of her German-speaking home, could almost believe that she'd stepped into that room a thousand times and never seen the picture, or not allowed herself to see it.

Soon, however, an image of the aged Tomas Masaryk, founder of Czechoslovakia, reassured her. In no way could this face, severe with its grey goatee beard and yet the raised right eyebrow suggesting the onset of a wistful smile, in no way could he be confused with the mad Nazi tyrant.

'There's a picture over the mantelpiece but it's not Hitler,' she said and despite her realisation that an explanation was a waste of time, she added, 'It's Masaryk. He used to be President of Czechoslovakia. Tommy was called after him.'

'And what's more,' Mags continued defensively, 'you're like the gypsies, picking berries along the road and fighting like tinkers.'

'You never used to say things like that to me, Mags,' Lida retorted. 'Someone's been poisoning your mind.'

And even as Mags stuttered her denials, the identity of that 'someone' was obvious to Lida.

'Ginny Stannix,' she said.

Mags had never been good at hiding things and she was no better now.

'She told you all this, didn't she?'

'It's none of your business *who* told me,' Mags cried. 'Anyway, you're just jealous of her 'cause she's rich and she has everything she ...'

'At least I don't have a mad uncle climbing trees,' Lida shouted, and almost choked on the feeling of revulsion that came with dragging that poor, harmless man into her argument.

'Hubert Stannix is a war hero, just like Ginny's father,' Mags answered. 'If he's mad it's because of you Germans.'

'I'm not German. How many times do I have to tell you?'

'My lunch is ready. I have to go in.'

The door banged in her face and through the glass panel Lida saw Mags running to her mother in tears. Sick with hate, Lida walked between the pretty pansies along the path to the gate. But it wasn't Mags she hated and, for now, it wasn't her father.

It was Ginny Stannix.

She would have her revenge on the tennis court. She'd thrash her, beat her to a pulp, humiliate her. From now on she'd practice every last second of every possible hour at the club. Even if it meant licking up to Mrs Mackey. If she needed any further spur to her renewed vigour it came a few days later with the draw for the second round of the championship.

Her opponent was to be none other than the gossip-monger – the story-carrier – Ginny Stannix's servile messenger girl: Mags Campion.

CHAPTER 9

A sullen pall hung over the dinner table that first evening after Tommy had left. None of them had any appetite for the goulash Anna had made. This spicy stew was her speciality and she'd often told Lida of the Hungarian neighbour who'd taught her how to make it.

The woman, Magda, had married a young man from Anna's village who'd died a year after her only child was born. Magda had been left alone, a stranger in the village and Anna had befriended her. When Anna had come to Ireland, leaving Magda had been almost worse than saying goodbye to her own ageing parents. Now, it was Anna who was the stranger in a place still unfamiliar after so many years. A stranger at her own table at a time like this, for all three of them were lost in their separate solitudes.

So far from one another were they that even their thoughts revealed themselves in different languages. Lida considered the problems with her backhand in her terse English. Her mother repeated the many words and phrases of Hungarian she'd learnt from Magda. Her father wondered, in his dour Low German accent, whether he should tell them of the latest possibility that had opened up to him.

The kettle on the range lifted its lid every now and then and dropped it down with a metallic crash in protest at the silence. On the street outside, a hay lorry passed and sent grinding vibrations through the walls of the house. But the house refused to be shocked back into life. Josef Hendel sighed into his teacup. His warm breath mingled with the steam from the tea and lent his face a sheen of beady moisture. He wiped the moisture away and rubbed it between his fingers.

'There's something I have to tell you,' he announced, at last.

Hoping against hope, Lida was putting words into his mouth: 'I've decided to take the new house.' She dropped the racket in her mind. Her mother waved goodbye to Magda in hers.

'I've just been told there's a job for me down at our factory in Mallow if I want to take it.'

'Mallow?' Anna exclaimed.

'It's down south, about sixty miles from here,' he said, 'in County Cork.'

'I know where it is. But why?'

He shrugged his shoulders almost disinterestedly and leaned his chin on his hand.

'It would be a new start for us,' he answered. 'Maybe that's what we need.'

Anna looked down at her plate, momentarily disappointed, but quickly raised her head and smiled.

'Yes, why not?' she said. 'We should think about it, yes.'

'Lida?' he asked, addressing her directly for the first time in days.

Her foolish expectations come to nothing, Lida hadn't the heart for any more conflict. In any case, she thought, this town had little to offer her now. If they left she wouldn't even have a Magda to part sadly with.

'*Es ist mir egal*,' she said. 'I don't mind. How soon would it be?'

'Not for a month or two,' he told her, a sense of certainty in his voice now that he had their agreement. 'It might be just the thing to …'

He reached across to the shelf where the radio stood and switched it on.

'It's always so quiet here,' he noted good-humouredly. 'Why do you never have some music going?'

He turned the volume knob clockwise as Lida and her mother exchanged concerned glances. They both knew he was the one who never wanted the radio on. There was something unnatural and worrying about his cheerfulness. When they heard the music whistling into earshot, they knew what to expect.

The radio was tuned to AFN, American Forces Network. This was Tommy's favourite station, where he listened to the swing music of the Big Bands – the music he and the other members of The Silver Sound tried to recreate in their own small way. A casual, mellow voice crooned soft words that sounded more sneering than sincere.

Very calmly Josef Hendel picked up his knife and scraped it along the rim of his plate to remove the remnants of goulash. He turned to the radio and plunged the knife through the dull, brass-coloured mesh of its front. After one more stab, something shattered crystal-like inside and the music died. He replaced the knife and stood up. The look of grief on his face was so shattering that Lida and her mother, as if in a practised move, both raised their left hands over their downcast eyes.

'I'm sorry,' he said. 'I'm very sorry.'

Just go, Lida screamed silently, go before you aim the knife at us.

'It's just a valve,' he muttered, 'I'll get a new one in O'Brien's … tomorrow.'

He placed his finger in the open-lipped cuts on the radio mesh. Lida felt such pain, he might just as well have been fingering the wound in her heart.

'No harm done,' he sighed. 'Tomorrow ... a new valve ...'

He brought himself to the kitchen door, faltered and went out.

'Mama,' Lida whispered, 'he's mad.'

'Not mad, child,' her mother said, 'just very sad.'

'How can you tell the difference?' Lida asked, but her mother made her no answer.

When the day of the second round came, Lida's nerves were near to breaking point. Her renewed determination to win, frightening in its intensity, had, if anything, increased her fear of losing. Defeat was now the stuff of her recurrent nightmares.

Each night she dreamed of being beaten, not by Mags or by Ginny or any of the other girls, but by a demented Mrs Mackey, who leaped around in her fussy tweed suit. It should have been funny but instead it was terrifying. Sometimes she returned Lida's shots not with a racket but with a knife and sometimes instead of a tennis ball it was the paperweight from Mrs Mackey's desk that came flying at Lida's face.

The promise of an end to her days in town was also tainted by fear. Her father hadn't changed, might never change, and life would be just as miserable wherever they went.

And there was her racket. Always that awful racket. Taking the joy and confidence from her play.

All of these things, heaped together like a barricade to happiness, contributed to her losing the first set in her game with Mags Campion. All of these things and Ginny too, sitting primly on the bench by the pavilion alongside Mrs Mackey.

'Wonderful shot!' Mrs Mackey would exclaim and, touching Ginny's hand, add, 'The things you've done to improve that girl's game. It's beyond me. Beyond me!'

For the moment, it was beyond Lida too. Many of
Mags's shots still sailed into the sky but with more control
now. Lida had let several of them pass over her head in the
early stages of the match, expecting them to come to
ground in the next field. As she turned time and again,
however, she watched in amazement as the ball dipped
and bounced just short of the end line.

The second set was well under way before Lida recov-
ered sufficiently to figure out what was happening. Then
it came to her. She was rushing to the net too quickly after
her serves and returns.

This was the serve and volley game of her tennis
heroines, those aggressive Americans who'd taken
Wimbledon by storm in the years since the war had ended.
The English players, with their more ladylike style, were
no match for the likes of Dupont, Hart, Brough and Todd,
this year's Wimbledon semi-finalists.

Up to now, the sight of Lida serving strongly and advancing like a sprinter off the blocks had always confused her
opponents. She'd be so near the net they couldn't imagine
getting the ball past her. But there was a way. Lida wasn't
tall so the trick was to get it high over her and have it drop
suddenly behind her.

There was no question as to whether Mags had figured
this out for herself. It had to be Ginny's idea. That the
blonde girl had seen the flaw in her game made Lida feel
desperately vulnerable. Changing her style of play proved
to be a monumental task. It called for a patience which she
had little of. Staying at the base line was, at first, almost
impossible for her to do. The net was like a magnet to her.

By and by, however, she rooted herself to the line and
found she was edging her way back into the match. Mags
was coming under pressure and she looked in desperation
to Ginny after each lost point. When the second set ended
in Lida's favour, Mags ran to her new friend and they

whispered intently to each other for all of five minutes. Mrs Mackey too had some muted words of advice for the sweat-drenched girl.

Lida was incensed. She'd worked hard to find some rhythm in her play, even if it was an unfamiliar one. The long break threatened to undo all her efforts.

'Do you mind if we finish the match,' she called to the conspiring trio, 'today?'

'Mind your tongue,' Mrs Mackey sniped. 'You need to learn how to take your beating.'

'I'm not being beaten.'

'Not yet,' Mrs Mackey gloated. 'Not yet.'

Moving back into position on court, Mags seemed reassured. For the first time since the match had begun their eyes met. Mags looked as if she had another surprise up her sleeve. A new game plan to counteract Lida's end-line tactic, no doubt.

The last thing Mags would expect, Lida guessed, would be to see her charge the net again. Ginny had obviously told her to play a different kind of shot. Returning to her normal game, Lida reckoned, would throw Mags into confusion. Her reckoning was correct. Lida had gone 4–1 up before Mags had figured out that her low tophand volleys were playing into her opponent's hands.

With every shot, Lida grunted and groaned more and more aggressively, punishing the big girl mercilessly for her treachery. But the force of Lida's vengeance became too great for her racket to bear. She met Mags's return of service with such brute power that the timber in her hand cracked and sang its destruction into the bones of her fingers. The ball sank into the net and the stringed oval of her racket dropped at her feet. She looked in disbelief from Mags to Ginny to Mrs Mackey and back at the stalk of split timber in her fist.

Mrs Mackey advanced towards her, looking pleased.

'It seems the match is over for you, Miss Hendel,' she said.

'I'll get a loan of a racket from someone.'

'From whom?' the club secretary inquired. 'Do you have anyone you can ask?'

Lida looked round the handful of spectators and knew there wasn't one amongst them who'd be willing to help her. Or, at least, none she'd be willing to ask.

'You have some rackets in your office,' Lida said.

'Isn't it a pity I left the key at home now,' she replied, but turning to go found her departure blocked by a glowing white vision.

'Would you like to use one of these?' Ginny asked, holding up her two Blue Flash rackets.

The choice for Lida was a stark one: humble herself by accepting the offer, or bow out of the championship. Or was there, perhaps, a possible compromise?

'It wouldn't be fair to Mags,' Lida protested. 'Her old racket is worse than mine. Give her yours and I'll take hers.'

'I'm not Josie Hayes,' Mags called from the other side of the net. 'I don't need excuses. My racket is grand.'

'Really, Miss Stannix,' Mrs Mackey objected, 'this isn't at all necessary.'

'Do take it,' Ginny insisted, 'please.'

The memory of those spiteful accusations, relayed through Mags, returned as Lida faced the one who was, without doubt, responsible. How could someone talk like that behind your back and then make this showy gesture? And why make it? Because she knew Lida would have to refuse?

Staying in the competition was Lida's only way of getting even. In the last half-hour she had learned a little of the benefits of patience. This was the time to apply that lesson. She took the new racket from Ginny's hand.

'Thank you very much,' she said with all the politeness she could muster.

Ginny returned to the bench, betraying no surprise at having had her offer accepted. Mrs Mackey grabbed Lida's arm tightly.

'That is how a real lady behaves,' she whispered and trotted away demurely to take her place beside her gracious guest.

The match continued and within five minutes, Lida was 5–1 up and leading 30–love. Mags was in disarray. Her blouse hung out over her skirt and as she stretched to each shot, the rippling folds of flesh on her belly were exposed for all to see. Lida was glad she'd got a white blouse of her mother's on, even if it was a few sizes too big.

In the small crowd someone began to titter, another guffawed loudly. Lida knew Mags was the object of their mirth. The rage seeped from her play and attached itself to the sneering pair of boys, the same ones who'd tried to make fun of her on the day of her suspension.

It was Lida's serve. The two boys had edged closer to the sideline to get a better view of Mags. By now they knelt halfway along the side Lida was to serve to. She had to admit to herself that Ginny's racket gave a whole new dimension to her already powerful serve. For now, she was glad of it.

Summoning up every last ounce of malicious strength in her small, wiry frame she aimed her service directly at the red-haired one, the one with the loud guffaw. He'd already swivelled his head to see Mags's raised blouse when the ball, without a bounce, met his left ear. He stood up, swayed drunkenly and flopped to the grass like a puppet whose strings have been shorn.

'The doctor's son!' Mrs Mackey screeched. 'Lord bless us and save us, is he dead?'

Panic-stricken, Lida imagined the worst. Her menacing

German streak had driven her to murder or, at the very least, to the cracking of a skull. She was going to be sick, she was sure of it. But the boy's mealy-mouthed yelps intruded and the surge of self-hate ebbed away.

'She meant it,' he cried. 'She bloody well meant it.'

Then another voice interjected to Lida's astonishment.

'You were too near the court,' Ginny Stannix intoned with quiet authority.

Mrs Mackey was in a tizzy. How to choose between the doctor's son and the beautiful young protégé of Stannix House?

'Perhaps you were, James,' she stuttered, 'a trifle too near. But I ask you, is there any call for hitting a ball as hard as that?'

Needing only two more points to win the match, Lida felt Mags had suffered enough and deliberately mis-hit her next two shots. She needed to prove to herself that this racket wasn't perfect, though she'd hardly lost a point since taking it up. However, both shots somehow stayed inside the line to Lida's consternation. The match was over. She'd achieved what she'd set out to, the annihilation of her former friend. But the victory left a sour taste.

The first person to shake her hand after Mags's indifferent congratulation was Ginny. Lida was no longer surprised by the girl's two-faced brazenness. She handed the racket back but Ginny didn't take it.

'Would you like to keep it?' she asked. 'It seems just right for you.'

Surrounded by the knot of curious bystanders, Lida was like a poker player with a losing hand. To accept would be to surrender every last shred of her dignity. To refuse would deepen the hostility of those around her. She tried to manoeuvre her mind through the small space left between these two alternatives.

'I couldn't really,' she said. 'I'll probably be getting a

new one now anyway.'

'But you must take it,' Ginny declared ever so cheer-fully. 'It was *made* for you.'

Deciding that her own self-respect was more important than the opinions of others she pushed the racket at Ginny.

'I ... don't ... want ... it,' she said, each word more heavily accented than the next in its clinical finality.

As she extracted herself from the disbelieving crowd, she saw Ginny shrug her shoulders, the beginnings of a grin playing at the corner of her mouth.

'Don't you dare laugh at me,' Lida exclaimed, 'and let me tell you I have nothing to hide. Not in my house ... or in the trees around my house.'

Ginny swallowed hard not to lose the twisted smile on her face. Her refusal to be drawn into an argument maddened Lida even more. It was as if she was suggesting that Lida was too contemptible to bother with.

'Well, really,' Mrs Mackey tut-tutted.

'Ah, feck off,' Lida muttered and retreated towards the pavilion shamefacedly.

'What did she say?' the club secretary cried.

'I'm afraid I didn't hear,' Ginny said, but Lida was already in the solitary shaded comfort of the pavilion's interior.

She dressed quickly but found she couldn't face the hostile group outside just yet. The soft, puttering echo of play reached through her addled thoughts. Ginny's match, she knew, had begun. Her opponent, Kay Rafferty, was a thirteen-year-old and this was her first championship. She was nimble on her feet but smaller even than Lida. Mrs Mackey's 'fair draw' had been kind to Ginny Stannix.

Lida hoped that the young girl might, at least, take a few games but even this faint wish was quashed when one of the other competitors entered the dressing room.

'The first set is over already,' the girl said.

Lida knew she was telling her this simply to intimidate her. Normally the girl wouldn't have spoken to Lida at all. Grabbing the remains of her racket, Lida left the dressing room and sucking in a deep breath went outside.

'Four games to one,' someone said, clearly in awe of the club's new favourite.

'And she let Kay win that one,' another piped up. 'It was sticking out a mile.'

Never having seen Ginny in a real match, Lida wanted to stay on and study her style. However, she was so sickened by the blonde girl's sympathetic attitude to Kay Rafferty that she couldn't bear to watch.

'Oh, bad luck,' Ginny called after a near-miss by her opponent. 'It really should have gone in, you hit it so well.'

Kay herself, no less than Ginny's enthusiastic following, was taken in by the pretence. Gasps of admiration, bursts of applause, sighs of devotion, filled the club grounds as Lida walked unnoticed through the lane to the street.

A time would come, Lida convinced herself, when they would see Ginny for what she really was. For now, the broken racket in her hand offered a faint glimmer of hope.

Surely her father would agree to buy her a new racket now? No longer would she have to present him with vague complaints about the racket's age. It was broken and would have to be replaced. It was as simple as that.

CHAPTER 10

'*Mein Schläger ist gebrochen*,' Lida told her father as he unscrewed the back of the radio.

He began to pick out the icicle-like shards of valve glass from the dusty depths, ignoring her all the while.

'My racket is broken,' she repeated.

His hand shot back from its careful explorations. A droplet of blood glistened on his upraised finger. He pointed it at her as if she was to blame.

'You're always complaining about that racket,' he said firmly. 'It's old but there's nothing wrong with it.'

Lida went out into the hallway and reached into the cubby-hole under the stairs where she'd left the wreckage. When she returned he was hunched over the radio again. She placed the sundered timbers on the table and he considered them doubtfully.

'It's in bits,' she declared. 'Do you believe me now?'

He raised himself from his kneeling position, the screwdriver still in his hand.

'You did this deliberately, didn't you?' he said.

'It happened during a match,' she snapped back. 'You can ask Mrs Mackey if you like. She was there.'

'Yes,' he said, 'I will ask Mrs Mackey.'

Sweeping her hand across the table Lida sent the racket hurtling through the kitchen. The cracked handle smashed into the oven door, knocking a chip from its cream-coloured enamel. The stringhead clattered into the sink, turning the tap to a weak dribble as it went.

The back door opened just as Josef threw down his screwdriver. Lida stood rooted to the spot but she wasn't afraid. Rather, she was wondering quite coldly and calmly whether her father dared cross the ever narrowing dividing line between cruel words and violent actions. He hesitated, his cheeks burning like a boy's, caught out in some mischief-making.

'She … she …' he muttered.

'He was going to hit me, Mama,' she countered. 'I stood up to him and he acted like a typical German. He tried to lash out at me.'

'Lida,' her mother protested. 'How dare you speak of your father like that!'

'Why does he pretend to be an innocent Czech?' Lida demanded of her mother. 'Why doesn't he put Hitler's ugly face up on the wall instead of Masaryk?'

Josef Hendel retreated to the kitchen door. His mouth moved dumbly. He was having trouble catching his breath.

'All you can do is run away,' Lida said. 'Like you run away from everything else. The new houses … and now you want to go to Mallow, as if that will solve anything.'

'Stop it, Lida,' her mother warned as her father gathered up his coat in the hallway and left the house.

'Coward,' Lida shouted. 'Miser! *Heil Hit* …'

The sting of her mother's slap burst open Lida's tear ducts. Her hand trembled to feel the blazing wetness in her cheek. She searched for some sign of regret in her mother's face and found none. She'd never seen her mother look so severe, and was more afraid of her now than she was of her father.

'Mama,' she whimpered, 'he tried to make a liar of me. He wouldn't believe my racket was broken in the match.'

'I never want to hear you speak like that to him again,' her mother retorted. 'How many men, do you think, in this street, in this town, would allow a daughter to behave as you've just done? In any other home you would have been beaten. Do you imagine I could ever have spoken to my father in such a way? Do you?'

'He wouldn't listen to me. He ...'

'Let me tell you how it was for Josef at your age. Whipped by his father because of his stepmother's lies, blamed for every single thing that went wrong on the farm. You want to know what madness is, what evil is? What it's really like to be unloved, uncared for?'

Lida stared as her mother's face became disfigured by a nightmarish indignation.

'When he told me this story, Lida, he was twenty-five years old and he cried in my arms.'

The painful image of her young parents shocked and embarrassed Lida. She averted her eyes as if this might make her mother's anguish easier to bear.

'He was thirteen. It was winter and the snows were deep,' Anna began. 'Josef walked in by the lane to the farmhouse and Frieda was waiting in the yard. He was late home from school. In his absence three cattle had got loose and his father had had to go and find them. Something Josef would normally have had to do. He hadn't noticed the cold until he'd seen her but now he trembled, trembled even as he told me about it all those years later. She was a big, rough woman and standing there with her strong arms folded, chewing on the remains of her dinner, she fixed her huge, bovine eyes on him as he came near. Just as he drew level she spat. He could feel the droplets of spittle on his lips as he stared at the dark, phlegmy spit burning like acid into the white snow. That's what it's like to be despised in your own home, Lida.'

'I'm sorry,' Lida said weakly.

'I'm the one who should be sorry,' her mother said. 'I should never have hit you. Your father would never have done that.'

'It's all right.'

Her cheek, bearing the imprint of her mother's fingers, had gone quite numb. The unbidden tears had dried. The dark kitchen slowly eased itself back into equilibrium. Anna drummed the table with her fingertips with a mounting rhythm. She eased back her chair and rose. Lida was surprised by the sudden flash of resolve on her mother's face.

'There's something I want you to do for me, Lida.'

The agonised atmosphere had evaporated. In its place, a sense of renewed purpose wafted through the cramped space.

'I want you to go to Ger Kinsella's and tell Tommy he's to come here for his dinner after his father has gone back to work. Every day. Will you do that?'

'Of course,' Lida declared.

'And Lida …'

'Yes?'

'You will have your new racket,' her mother told her, 'tomorrow.'

Walking towards Kickham Street, Lida was sure a turning point had been reached in the crisis at Garravicleheen. Defying the huge waves of fate, her mother was steering the small boat that was the Hendel family towards some shoreline. A shoreline that only she could see and Lida merely imagine. A shoreline whose existence her father and Tommy were not even aware of, so busy were they with the feud that threatened to ditch all of them in the merciless waters.

The broad grey plaza of the town square was usually subdued on Wednesday afternoons, its shops closed for the 'half-day'. However, as soon as she turned the corner from Friary Street, Lida could hear a commotion at the far end. In the distance, the children's raised voices seemed innocent enough. It was unusual to see so many of them, twenty, perhaps even thirty, playing together on the square.

As she approached, their screeches seemed to grow more hysterical. Something sinister in their high-pitched calls reminded her of a flock of crows disturbed from their nesting tree. Then she heard what it was they were half-shouting, half-singing:

'Loony! Loony! Put him in the loony bin!'

They pointed at the doorwell of Flynn's Drapery Shop and took turns running towards it and skittering back to the safety of the flock. Little more than a few inches from the ground, a hand reached out around the corner of the doorwell, beating at the air, pleading, holding on desperately to the wall.

'Leave him alone!' Lida shouted and swung her fists, making contact with two or three of the delirious mob as she swept through.

One of them yelped and charged at Lida but she pushed him back so hard that he hit the ground and smacked his head on the pavement. The others went quiet, gathered up their ringleader and began to shuffle away, along by the Blackcastle Bridge.

'I'll tell me oul' fellow on you!' the injured boy yelled, his face looking like it hadn't seen soap for a month. 'He'll drag your dirty black head off you!'

'Go home and wash yourself!' Lida shouted.

She edged towards the huddled unfortunate, guessing it was some poor, befuddled tramp who'd wandered into town. He had his back to her, his hands still covering his grey head.

'Why?' the man whimpered. 'Why?'

His voice was unexpectedly young. He squirmed away from her touch and made himself smaller again, more invisible.

'It's all right,' she said. 'I only want to help you.'

She knew that if she could get him up to the County Home that the nuns there would look after him, give him something to eat and a bed for the night.

'Will you let me help you?' she asked. 'I can take you to …'

She froze. The man had turned suddenly to look at her. It was Hubert Stannix, the tree-climbing uncle of her worst enemy. She put all thought of Ginny to the back of her mind as she lifted him from the cold tiles of the doorwell. It was the least she felt she could do after using him, as she had done so cruelly, as ammunition in her cold war with Ginny.

'I ran out of petrol,' he explained, peering round in confusion. 'I came into town to get … something … something …. Yes, something for Rose. Something Rose asked me to get … I think.'

'Where's the car, Mr Stannix?'

'The car? Where's the car?' he repeated, trying to make sense of the question.

Lida felt trapped. How could she leave him in this state? But how too could she help him if he couldn't remember where he'd left the car? She looked along the length and breadth of the square but the unmistakable blue car was nowhere to be seen. Maybe Tommy would know what to do.

'My brother lives up in Kickham Street,' she told Hubert. 'He'll help you find it.'

He nodded but she wasn't sure if he understood a word she'd said. She took his arm half-expecting some resistance. There was none. Heading over Blackcastle Bridge, she found herself flushed with embarrassment as people passed by, unable to contain their curiosity. Along Church

Street she cursed herself for having got involved at all and cursed herself too for being ashamed at her simple act of kindness.

There was some relief for her when she reached Church Lane and the nosy old woman was absent from her post at the half-door. Hubert spoke every now and then but only to himself. Lida said nothing at all. The blue door of Ger Kinsella's house was open when she got there. Stepping inside she prayed that Tommy would be in.

From the kitchen at the end of the hall, Ger, red-faced and baggy-eyed, appeared. The light from the street outside showed the true extent of disrepair the house had fallen into. Ger's state of degradation was no less plain to see. His face was stained with purple blotches and his teeth, brown from cigarettes and stout, seemed to rot even as he smiled at her.

'Well, girl,' he said. 'Are you looking for the young lad?'

'Is he here?' she asked sharply.

'He is indeed,' Ger said and called back to the kitchen. 'Tommy! You have a visitor.'

Tommy looked in better shape than he'd done on her last visit. The look of surprise at seeing Hubert Stannix with her seemed to make his face younger, more like the brother she knew.

'Mr Stannix needs a hand to find his car,' she said, realising how ridiculous she sounded. 'Some young fellows were giving him a hard time on the square and he got … a little mixed up.'

They brought him into the kitchen and Lida gagged on the foul-smelling air. The one window, she noticed, was nailed in place and the crack on the glass pane wasn't wide enough to let in more than a useless wisp of freshness. Stale bread-crumbs littered the table. Half-empty milk bottles stood forlornly by the sink, their contents stinking to the heights. Tommy saw her eyes fall on the bottles.

'Ger keeps the sour milk for Mrs Kennedy next door,' he explained, 'for the soda bread, you know.'

'I live on the stuff,' Ger confessed and, pointing to a chair, added, 'Sit down there for yourself, Mr Stannix. There's tea in the pot.'

His crusty cheerfulness puzzled Lida. She couldn't understand how he could seem so at ease with himself knowing, as he surely must, how pathetic a sight he presented. She wiped some crumbs from a chair and sat beside Hubert.

'Where am I?' Hubert asked, his voice firm but his hands shaking too much to hold the stained mug of tea Ger had placed before him.

'You're at the Kinsella residence, Mr Stannix,' Ger said. 'Take a good sup there and you'll be right as rain in no time.'

The pale brown liquid spilled over the rim of the mug as Hubert drank. Rivulets of tea trickled along the sides of his chin but he didn't appear to notice.

'I'm not mad, you know,' Hubert said, 'I'm … I'm out of touch … I seem to be very far away from …'

Lida looked at Tommy. He hunched his shoulders as if to confirm that he was as much at a loss to know what the man was trying to say as she was.

'I know the feeling,' Ger said and Lida glared at him, thinking he was trying to be sarcastic.

He clearly wasn't. He too was drifting away into his own thoughts. It was a peculiarly familiar scene for Lida. Four people sitting at a table and only two of them, herself and Tommy, really there in spirit.

'Can you remember where you left the car?' Tommy asked.

For all its filth and decay, Lida felt a human warmth permeate the kitchen.

'Hubert. Call me Hubert.'

'We'll find it, Hubert,' Tommy smiled. 'We couldn't miss that big blue yoke.'

'It's because of Bobby ... my brother Bobby,' Hubert mumbled, adrift again. 'No one deserves to die like that.'

The last thing Lida wanted to hear about was war and killing and Nazi stormtroopers. She hadn't rescued Hubert to be reminded of that again.

'So ... so cheap and nasty ... to go like that after all he'd been through,' he continued, 'and no one ... not one of his own with him ... all twisted up in that car ... the city ... I dream about it ... I can't stop dreaming about it ...'

He raised a hand to his mouth as if to stop the flow of words that should never have been spoken. The others set their mugs on the table. Lida worried some crumbs into a ball with her fingers. They all knew some dark secret had raised its ugly head from the torment of Hubert's mind.

Everyone in town knew the story of Captain Robert Stannix's death. His wife, Rose, had trumpeted it often enough to anyone who was prepared to listen. Leading his men into a quiet village, its few buildings pock-marked from shell-bursts, he was hit by a sniper's bullet and lay dying as another unit, led by Hubert, rushed to their assistance. Robert had died in his brother's arms and the legend was born.

But what was this talk of 'a car', 'a city', of 'none of his own' being with him? Lida was certain of one thing, though and that was the fearful ring of truth in Hubert's mangled words. She thought of Ginny, of the possibilities that knowing this secret would offer in her continuing battle with her. Watching Hubert's nerve-shot hand-wringing, however, brought her to her senses and she dismissed the unworthy thought.

'I should be getting home,' he said and then added brightly, a problem solved, 'Parnell Street.'

'Parnell Street?' Ger muttered. 'I thought you lived on

the Cormackstown Road.'

'The car,' Lida explained.

'Stay right where you are, Mr Stannix,' Ger announced, on his feet in an instant. 'I'll get the car for you. Take your time drinking the tea there.'

'There's no petrol in it,' Lida told him.

'Not to worry,' Ger said. 'I'll get some from Mick Sullivan in Dwan's yard. Have you the keys?'

'I'm afraid I left them in the car,' Hubert said. 'Foolish of me.'

'No harm done,' Ger laughed. 'Sure, who'd feck a car you couldn't hide?'

When Ger left, neither Tommy nor Lida could think of any subject for idle talk to pass the time until he returned. Hubert took another sip from the clay-coloured mug. He grimaced.

'Pretty awful stuff, isn't it?' he smiled. 'But, you know, I think I could get used to it.'

'Believe me,' Tommy groaned, 'you never would.'

'I like that fellow. Ger, is it? He's a decent chap. And you two, of course. I want to thank you for …'

Again a silence fell on the kitchen and Lida grew more and more uncomfortable. Thoughts of Ginny and revenge and betrayal of a disturbed man's trust sent her mind spinning. She had to leave before some stupidly cruel question passed her lips and Hubert was thrown once again into the maelstrom of ravaged memory.

'I have to go home,' she said. 'Mama wants me to do some ironing.'

Tommy shot her an impatient, warning glance but she ignored it.

'Mama says you're to come up for your dinner after Papa goes back to work.'

'I don't know,' Tommy answered, not happy to be talking about the Hendel's problems in front of a stranger.

'I'm just delivering the message,' Lida continued. 'If you want to be pig headed, that's your own business. Goodbye, Mr Stannix.'

'Goodbye and again, many thanks,' he said, moving awkwardly from his chair and bowing just as awkwardly.

Tommy glared at her, nodding towards Hubert who was trying hard not to notice. She went out and when she reached the front door she heard Tommy call after her.

'I'll come. Tell Mama, I'll come.'

Back in the square, she waved as Ger Kinsella drove contentedly by in the plush Delage, blowing the klaxon and singing loudly to himself above the burr of the engine. His clear musical timbre surprised her as much as his sympathy and fellow-feeling for Hubert. She knew she had too easily passed judgement on him, had believed the malicious gossip of others. Had she, perhaps, judged Ginny too harshly as well? She thought not. The arrogance and deceit of that girl were plain to see. Nothing could excuse them. Not the troubled presence of her uncle or this half-revealed family secret. There was no mellowing of Lida's feelings for Ginny as there was for Ger Kinsella. She was unrelenting in her desire to destroy the perfect white-haired girl.

And tomorrow she would have the stick to beat her with. A new tennis racket.

CHAPTER 11

The sign over the shop door read 'O'Donnell's Jewellers', but inside among the gold and silver rings and necklaces, the cut glass ornaments and porcelain figures, were treasures of far more value to Lida. This place, oddly enough, was the best in town when it came to buying a tennis racket and much else besides jewellery. It was a favourite haunt of Tommy's, as they also had the best collection of 78 records around.

When Mrs O'Donnell saw Lida and her mother enter the shop she stooped down to search under the counter.

'You've come for Tommy's record,' she declared, sounding somewhat relieved. 'I've been holding it for ages.'

'No,' Anna Hendel said, unaware as ever of the cold impression her accent left.

'It's that Django Reinhardt one he was looking for,' the woman continued, raising her head above the counter. '"Honeysuckle Rose". You might tell him it's in.'

To Mrs O'Donnell, Anna's silence seemed an uncalled-for stubbornness. Anna however, was simply trying to put a phrase of English together and, shy as ever, found herself unable to say it once it finally took shape in her mind. Lida came to her rescue.

'We'd like to see some tennis rackets, Mrs O'Donnell,' she said and the woman brightened considerably.

A wide array of rackets was laid out on the glass-topped counter. Prices, weights and balances considered, Lida decided, at her mother's insistence, not on the cheapest racket but on one that was not too much more expensive. Even as Mrs O'Donnell wrapped the purchase in brown paper, Lida tried to avoid glancing at the more pricey rackets, especially the coveted Blue Flash. The kind Ginny Stannix had not one but two of, the kind which had felt so good in her hand during the match with Mags.

By the time they'd left the shop Lida had banished these ungrateful longings altogether. The fact that her mother had bought the racket at all was more important than how good or bad it was, more important than any junior championship title if it came to that.

Besides, it was without doubt a good racket. More than good, it was a thing of beauty to her. The taut catgut bounced away from her fist as she'd tested it in the shop. The weighty swing was easy on her wrist, which was strong from the three years spent lifting the old racket about in heavy arcs. It had a powerful, sweeping downward thrust as she mimed a serve, to the consternation of the shop owner who'd grabbed a crystal vase as though the thunderous breeze might send it crashing to the floor. Yes, it would do. It would do very well.

If she thanked her mother once on their homeward journey, she thanked her a hundred times. At first, the urgency of her gratitude came from the pure joy of this new possession. Soon, however, the reason for her repeated thanks changed. Her mother was quiet. Too quiet. Was she already regretting what she'd done behind her husband's back, Lida wondered?

'For the moment,' her mother said finally as they reached the front gate of the house, 'you'd better hide the racket from him.'

The package in her hands became a burden. It seemed

to her that every innocent pleasure had to be kept under wraps, obscured from her father's view: Tommy's music, her mother's listening to the radio, Lida's new racket. She followed her mother to the door wondering what lie she would have to tell her father to explain why she would still be playing in the championship – if he bothered to ask. In the hallway her mother was waiting for her, holding a letter she'd just picked up from the floor.

'It's for you.'

Lida took the unstamped envelope and opened it self-consciously as her mother watched. The delicately marbled notepaper was headed 'Stannix House'. Her eyes veered downwards to the signature, 'Mrs R.V. Stannix'. Lida stuffed the letter in her cardigan pocket. She'd seen not a word of what was written between the embossed heading and the precise signature but knew instinctively it spelt trouble.

'Who is it from?' her mother asked. 'Is there a secret admirer I should know about?'

Lida wasn't amused. It was no time for jokes.

'It's just a note from the tennis club.'

Her curiosity satisfied, Anna went along to the kitchen.

'I'll put the racket away under my bed,' Lida told her and trudged up the stairs to her room.

As she read the carefully constructed characters of Rose Stannix's script, Lida drew the loose-fitting cardigan, until recently her mother's, tightly to her front. This was not a letter written in some passion of grief. It was cold, calculated to wound.

'Dear Fraulein Hendel,' it began, 'I believe that is how you people like to be addressed. For my part, I will address you once and once only. I will thank you not to associate in any way, ever again, with my brother-in-law, Captain Hubert Stannix. He has already suffered a great deal and your intervention has not helped matters. However great his affliction, he is neither an invalid nor a simpleton and does not need the assistance of foreigners. I am sure that you and your family have, by now, derived much amusement from his unfortunate but temporary loss of faculties. However, I would ask you people to bear in mind which God-forsaken race it is which is responsible for his incapacity and for the untimely, murderous death of my dear husband, Captain Robert Stannix. If, by any chance, there is such a thing as a soul within the corrupt bodies of you Germans (and, frankly, I doubt it), I suggest that you search it, examine your consciences (again, no doubt, absent in your cases) and kindly refrain from tampering any further with lives you have already wilfully riven asunder. Yours faithfully, Mrs R.V. Stannix.'

When the metal tips of her father's working boots rang out in the hallway an hour later, the sheet of expensive paper was still in her hand. Twice she had crumpled it up only to tease it out and read again the savage diatribe. She thought about composing an equally nasty reply but the things that occurred to her to say were too confused to be written down. How could she explain the unique world of the Hendels when she couldn't make sense of it herself? Even if she could explain, Rose Stannix wouldn't want to understand.

In the end she decided that if war was what they wanted, then war was what they would get. She would fight on the battlefield that suited her best – the tennis court. She took the wrapping from her new racket and swung it around, getting the feel of it, smashing imaginary shots into Ginny's midriff. Dark nicknames for the perfect girl yelled themselves in her head, sounding somehow more sinister as they were transposed into German: *Der weisse Teufel, der schwarze Engel.* White Devil, Black Angel.

'Lida,' her mother called from below, dispelling the hell of her fury.

She stopped in mid-swing and saw herself in the mirror. Her teeth were bared, a nasty purple bloom suffused her cheeks, her eyes flashed like burning coals. She flung the racket on the bed and fumbled with the catch on the window, threw it open and swallowed great mouthfuls of clean air.

If this, her mirror image, was what others saw when she played, was it any wonder that she was so disliked? And if she and Ginny should meet in the championship final, wouldn't everyone imagine it to be a battle between good and evil? Ginny, composed as ever, in control of her emotions, would smile blandly. Lida, on the other hand, would be catty and aggressive and swear at every mistake. It was very obvious which roles the crowd would attach to each of them.

Descending the stairs, she knew that one wrong word from her father would cause her to explode. The story of his stepmother's cruelty had raised unanswerable questions in her mind.

How, when he had been treated so callously himself as a boy, could he behave so coldly towards his own son and daughter? Should he not have gone out of his way to make them happy after his own bleak experience? She recognised the selfishness of these thoughts but was certain that if she ever had children she would give them anything they wanted. There had to be a balance, of course, a child could be spoiled like Mags was. But Lida wouldn't believe she was demanding too much. To prove this she'd even convinced herself that she would willingly give back this new racket in exchange for the simple treasure of a normal home.

Josef and Anna were too busy chatting good-naturedly to notice Lida's state of tension-filled readiness. Taken aback by the light mood, Lida sat into her usual place at the table. She soon became irritated by their cheerful small talk and began to spread her mother's blackcurrant jam too thickly on a slice of home-made bread. This was often enough to send her father into one of his long tirades about wastefulness and greed. Now, however, he didn't appear to care.

When he turned to Lida it wasn't in anger.

'I have something for you,' he said and went out to the hallway.

For a mad instant, the almost laughable possibility suggested itself to her. He'd gone and bought her a new racket! She'd moved to wondering what to do with the one from O'Donnell's when a look from her mother made the fantasy dissolve. Anna's knitted brows spoke of warning.

Josef appeared at the door triumphantly bearing the old racket. It had miraculously come together again as in some irrational dream.

'I brought it up to Tom Holmes in Cuchulainn Road,' he announced. 'The man's a miracle worker.'

Under the table, her mother's foot rubbed against Lida's ankle. Once. And then again more urgently. Lida forced a smile across her dumbfounded features. A panic of words escaped her lips.

'It's ... thank ... I can't believe ... I can't believe it could ... it could be fixed.'

'I didn't have much hope for it myself,' he declared, taking his seat at the table and offering the racket to her. 'It just proves you can fix anything if you put your mind to it.'

Even the tattered remnants of a family, Lida asked herself? And the question must have shown in her expression because her mother's foot renewed its nudging below the table.

'I ... I can't wait to try it out,' she said, hating herself for having to hide behind lies but thinking that, at least, she wasn't doing it for her own sake.

'The draw for the quarter-final is the day after to-morrow,' she added, feigning enthusiasm. 'I don't know what I'd have done if I didn't have a racket.'

'Are you going to win the title again?' he asked brightly.

'Yes,' she said. 'I have to.'

Her father was puzzled by her vehemence.

'It's not always important to win, you know,' he advised. 'Don't be putting pressure on yourself.'

If an argument was what Lida wanted she had her opportunity now. He hadn't won his 'title', his little plot in Moravia, and he'd wallowed in the defeat ever since. But her mother's foot was busy again and Lida held her tongue.

'I'll just go and try it out,' she said, desperate to escape. 'I need all the practice I can get.'

Over the next week, Lida spent her time from early morning to late afternoon at the tennis club. Each day she brought both rackets with her and never used the old one. Still, it felt good to be carrying two rackets, even if one was a dud.

Finding a partner remained a problem but she got by, though it invariably meant sharing a silent, joyless court with some reluctant girl. Even the announcement of the quarter final draw failed to dampen her spirits.

Lida wasn't at all surprised to be drawn against Bríd Thompson. In fact, she'd half-expected it. Bríd was the second strongest junior player at the club, after Lida herself. The last time she'd played her, Bríd had won but that had been a challenge match. In a fair draw they wouldn't have met until at least the semi-final.

As the days passed, she was possessed by that feeling that comes during a match, when you've been struggling and struggling and the other girl is in command and suddenly it comes right for you and now she's the one doing all the chasing, and the dead calm inside makes you feel invincible. Nothing your opponent can do, no question asked of your ability, is impossible to answer.

When, three days before the quarter-final, her father's mood took yet another unpredictable downturn, Lida's reaction was controlled and decisive. There was no explosion of feeling, no tantrum, no burn of frustration turned on her too-patient mother. She simply took matters into her own hands.

His announcement that he'd decided against going to Mallow seemed, at first, a prelude to better news. The choice was, in Lida's view, a simple one. Leave town or settle here once and for all – by buying one of the new factory houses. Her mother's and Lida's own hopes briefly raised, Josef stunned them with his next decision.

He wouldn't be taking the new house either, he'd said. Too expensive, didn't trust the builders, the site was damp. Excuses flowed from him in a miserable attempt to fill a silence he hadn't anticipated. Fighting off objections he might have found it easier to cloud the real issue – his own failure to make a real choice. As Josef left the table it sounded like he was disputing his own motives with himself.

'You think I'm doing this for myself, don't you?' he asked accusingly.

They knew where he was going and what he would be doing now as they sat in the kitchen. His footsteps paced overhead in confirmation. They didn't need to be in his room to see the photograph in Josef's hand, eyes gorging themselves on the black and white symbol of his despair.

Later in the evening, Josef went out to the factory to meet an engineer down from headquarters in Dublin. Lida made an excuse to go to her room and left her mother listening to light opera music on the lacerated radio, whose sound was tainted now by a tinny vibration. On the up-stairs landing Lida took off her shoes and padded carefully into her parent's bedroom. Easing open the top left-hand drawer of the dresser she found the photograph.

Back in her own room, she considered the dull white façade of the tall but narrow house. At the bottom was an arched door leading to the wine cellar. Above were two long, curtained windows and in the space between the steeply-sloped roof verges, a small, solitary attic window.

There should have been a figure at this window, she imagined. Some sickly child confined to its room and gazing out at the landscape beyond the camera. But the dark window space was empty except for the dull blur on its top right hand corner. A reflection of the sun, perhaps, but a cold sun lost in the mist of memory.

She put the photograph under the bed alongside the new tennis racket. A strange word fastened itself on the stillness. *Die geheimnisse Versammlerin*. Lida Hendel – the secret-gatherer.

CHAPTER 12

The Saturday of the quarter-final failed to live up to expectations. Sunny weather was predicted but instead it remained overcast and stiflingly humid. The epic struggle against Bríd Thompson that Lida had imagined also failed to live up to its billing. Bríd had a heavy cold and coughed and sneezed her way fitfully through the match. Lida's own play was plain awful. Far from working miracles for her, the new racket seemed to possess all the grace of a sledgehammer. More than once she looked over to where the old one lay, but didn't allow herself to pick it up. Playing on the uneven surface of the Pit didn't help either, exaggerating their faults.

The victory that was supposed to make up for the past three days of tension at home left Lida more restless and dissatisfied than ever. Sitting on the pavilion steps waiting for Ginny's match to begin, she tried to make sense of the morning's dramatic events at Garravicleheen.

Lida couldn't understand why, in his state of anxiety over the missing photograph, he had never thought to blame her. At first, he was sure he'd mislaid it himself. Then he asked her mother if she mightn't have tidied it away somewhere. He was quite calm and reasonable about it until this morning. As for Anna, Lida couldn't decide whether she simply did not suspect her or whether, guessing the truth, she'd decided to ignore it.

When Josef arrived back from work only an hour after leaving, they both knew some unpleasantness would follow. He'd been told by a workmate that Tommy had been visiting the house every afternoon and had decided that his son was the culprit.

'I won't allow my son to starve,' Anna had insisted, avoiding altogether the question of the photograph.

'He no longer belongs in this house,' Josef told her.

'None of us belong in this house,' she'd answered bitterly, and the argument raged with such ferocity that Lida's admission simply would not come.

His fist banging the table had driven the words back into her mouth and her false courage of recent days withered. He was going up to Ger Kinsella's, he'd thundered, and no one would stop him. They didn't try. As soon as he was gone Lida had confessed everything.

'I'll go after him,' she cried.

'No,' her mother had told her, 'you'll stay here – and that God-forsaken photograph will stay under your bed.'

'But why?'

'Because it's time he began to forget and if he won't do it himself, he will have to be made to.'

'It'll only make him worse, Mama.'

'For a while, maybe,' her mother had said finally. 'This photograph is a crutch. He must learn to live without it.'

Waiting for his return, Anna and Lida prepared themselves for yet another of his furious assaults. But it hadn't come. Even the steely ring of his boots was somehow muted as he passed in by the hallway. He didn't stay long in the kitchen, just long enough to ask a favour of Lida.

'Go to Tommy after your match today,' he said and she was surprised he'd even remembered she was playing. 'Tell him he can come home. I don't want him living in those conditions.'

When Lida nodded her assent he'd thanked her very

formally, as if she were a complete stranger to him. It made her wonder if his suspicions had now fallen on her. Each time she considered using the old racket during the match with Bríd, she'd seen that fixed, considered stare and heard those cold words of thanks.

At the end of the lane opposite the main court, Ginny Stannix floated into view in all her angelic whiteness. She was to play Áine Ryan, who was probably the weakest of those left in the competition. Another easy win for Ginny was likely, sugared with sweet politeness towards her opponent. Moving about the court in the warm-up, Ginny betrayed no signs of what was to come.

Áine Ryan started impossibly well, breaking serve in the first game. Still, there was nothing to show that Ginny was feeling the strain. Her elegant backswing seemed as fluid as ever, her high, arching service style almost ballet-like in its seeming delicacy. However, for some inexplicable reason, the scores weren't coming to her. When she lost the first set her benign smile was unaffected.

As she clawed her way back into the match, Lida dismissed the notion that Ginny had let the girl win those opening games. Another shot missed, Ginny stood for half a minute, her eyes downcast. She seemed to be talking to herself when suddenly she raised her head and stared directly at Lida. Looking around to see if she was simply imagining this, Lida saw that she had become the focus of everyone's attention. It was as if Ginny, and now all the others, were blaming Lida for this dismal performance.

From that point on, despite a half-dozen more uncharacteristic blunders, Ginny took charge of the match. Áine Ryan wilted quickly and in twenty minutes it was all over. Sweeping past the applauding crowd, Ginny made for the pavilion. Lida stood up to go but as they passed each other by, Ginny spoke to her. There was no pretence of pleasantry now, only a curt command.

'I want a word with you,' she said, 'inside.'

'We have nothing to say to each other.'

'You may not have but I do.'

They stood face to face on the pebbled path by the pavilion. A group of girls gathered nearby to hear what was going on.

'Do you mind?' Ginny erupted. 'We're having a private conversation.'

The girls were shocked to see their heroine turn into a viper. They edged away and settled into a hushed debate, sending long questioning looks back at the quarrelsome pair.

'You've caused so much trouble in my house,' Ginny said, 'that my mother has taken to her bed again and Hubert is ... is not himself at all.'

'I helped your uncle,' Lida retorted, 'but I can tell you I'll never help him again.'

'Hubert doesn't need any help. He needs to be left alone by people like you.'

No longer aware of the curious onlookers, Lida had had enough of insults. She launched an attack but didn't go for the direct hit. She went about her counterthrust carefully, slowly, so as to make it hurt all the more.

'Your uncle was very grateful to me,' she began. 'We had a good chat. He told me a lot of things. He's a nice man.'

'He's mad!' Ginny cried, a terrible uncertainty fracturing her precise tones. 'What did he tell you? What did you talk about?'

Lida couldn't hold back from the last twisting of the knife. The pleasure was as great as it was short-lived.

'Your father,' she said.

Ginny was an unlovely wreck now. Her normal paleness gave way to an unearthly puce.

'What did he say about my father?'

'It was all a bit confused really,' Lida said. 'Something about a car and a city and being alone when he ...'

She'd said too much, had almost said, 'when he died,' and that would have been too cruel. She knew she had to stop but even if she'd gone on, Ginny wouldn't have heard. Fleeing in visible horror, Ginny pushed aside some young fellows strolling along the path and ran to the lane and beyond to where Hubert's blue car had just pulled up.

The sight of Hubert left Lida suffering a dreadful sense of remorse. Once again she'd used this man's unhappiness as a tool of revenge. Moving towards the exit she felt like a spider crawling heavily, gorged with the tasteless remains of a hapless insect.

She had reason to be glad of only one thing. Mrs Mackey hadn't been around. A longer suspension, perhaps even dismissal from the championship, would certainly have followed. When she arrived at Ger Kinsella's house she couldn't stomach Tommy's reluctant mumblings about taking up his father's offer.

'You're just as thick-headed as he is,' she raged.

'It was hard enough to make the break,' he reasoned. 'I can't just give in like this.'

There was something dispirited about Tommy as he paced the floor, hands deep in his trouser pockets. Gone was the talk of freedom and enthusiasm for music. He looked out by the cracked pane into the yard littered with mouldy green bread crusts, whiskey bottles and empty cigarette packets.

'We played at a carnival marquee last night,' he said distantly, 'and all they wanted was Irish music. Cashel sets and the flippin' "Walls of Limerick". And the tent leaked on top of us all night. It was the pits. We didn't even get paid.'

'So you weren't floating this time?'

'I was floating all right – in mud,' he sighed and, turning from the window, added: 'I'll come. I can't sleep here. He plays the trumpet half the night.'

Tommy went upstairs to fetch his belongings and she pottered around the kitchen for a while, trying to put some shape on the chaotic mess. The work, though pointless, kept her from dwelling on the sorry row at the tennis club. So busy was she that she didn't hear the front door open or notice Ger Kinsella standing behind her. When he cleared his throat, an empty milk bottle flew from her hand and crashed on to the window sill. He was all apologies.

'It's all right,' she told him. 'I must have been dreaming.'

'You shouldn't bother tidying up the place,' he said wanting, it seemed, to say more than what followed. 'Since the wife died, well … she always said I hadn't a hand on me.'

'I was just waiting for Tommy,' Lida explained. 'I thought I might as well make myself useful.'

Ger Kinsella sat down at the table and opened his *Irish Independent*, leaning his elbow carelessly into a heap of breadcrumbs Lida had swept into one corner. He didn't seem very interested in what he was reading. Lida wished Tommy would hurry up and rescue her.

'He's packing up, is he?' Ger asked, still bent over his newspaper.

'Papa said he could come home.'

'That's good,' he said. 'You only have the one father and mother and they'll be gone soon enough, God knows.'

Tommy sidled into the kitchen behind Ger, looking shamefaced.

'Ger …' he began.

'You're doing the right thing, boy,' Ger reassured him. 'Only don't let that old marquee put you off the music, sure you won't?'

'I suppose.'

'Tommy,' Ger said, laying his paper on the table, 'you're the best I ever heard. You'll go places. Don't think you'll go downhill like … like I did. This is nothing to do with music … what happened to me.'

He sank back into his chair as if a great weight had been lifted from his shoulders. For all his obese and purpled grotesqueness, Ger had, in his simple admission of human frailty, achieved in Tommy and Lida's eyes a heroic stature.

'You're a helluva guy, Ger Kinsella,' Tommy smiled.

'That fellow reads too many of those old American dime novels,' Ger told Lida with a chuckle. 'He thinks he's Humphrey Bogart.'

At the front door, Ger looked up and down as if hoping to find someone to take Tommy's place. Lida, seeing the street through his eyes, knew its emptiness and friendlessness.

'Don't forget the rehearsal tonight,' Ger reminded Tommy.

'I'll be there, don't you worry.'

'By the way, what'll I tell Hubert if he calls?'

'Tell him,' Tommy said uncertainly, 'tell him to call up to my place if he wants.'

Ger closed out the door and Lida could imagine him trudging back to his lonely, echoing kitchen and blowing some heart-rending tune on the trumpet. Some tune known only to himself, some tune no one else wanted to know. But the sad image was soon dislodged by her curiosity.

'What was all that stuff about Hubert Stannix?'

Tommy turned up the collar of his overcoat like his detective heroes always did. If he'd had a hat, he'd have pulled it down over his eyes.

'Ah, he's been calling to the house ever since you brought him up,' he replied. 'He likes to talk. He thinks I'm a good listener.'

'What does he talk about?' Lida asked, sure that she'd be better off not knowing.

'Just small talk. Music and stuff. He gave me some books.'

'Haven't you enough of those gangster books already?'

They had reached Blackcastle Bridge. Tommy set his suitcase down and sat on the low stone wall above the River Suir. Sitting alongside him, Lida tried to hide her annoyance. If Hubert had spoken to Tommy every day for a week he must have told him more about Robert Stannix's death. Her brother gazed at the slow water, considering its journey and his own.

'Hubert doesn't read much of that stuff,' he mused. 'He gave me this book called *Animal Farm* by an English fellow, George Orwell. All about what happens when people get too much power and abuse it. Except all the characters are animals.'

'Sounds wonderful,' Lida muttered, but Tommy didn't seem to notice her lack of enthusiasm.

'See, some of the pigs are in charge and there's a great line they use. "All animals are equal but some animals are more equal than others." What do you think of that? Good, isn't it?'

'It's about Mrs Mackey then?'

There was something forced about his laughter. His thoughts were clearly elsewhere, wondering, perhaps, whether he was doing the right thing by moving home. It seemed to Lida that when he stood up to go he might head in either direction, back to Kickham Street or on to Garravicleheen. She couldn't blame him for thinking neither destination was very attractive.

More often than not Tommy made a nuisance of himself when he was around her, but Lida had missed him. She could understand why Hubert enjoyed his company. Tommy had a kind of energy you could feel even when he was as downcast as today. He had a desire to get up and do things, to try new experiences, to pursue whatever daft notions came into his head. Lost as he was in the deadening chasm of the past, Hubert must have seen in Tommy the possibilities of a renewed interest in life. But she was jealous of Hubert too, because while he and Tommy had talked during the past week, she had been left alone.

That he had become so friendly with a member of the same family which had caused her so much pain added to her sense of jealousy.

'Or maybe that book is about Rose Stannix,' she said and for a moment he looked askance at her, having already forgotten what it was they'd been talking about.

'Oh, the animals. Right,' he said. 'What made you mention her?'

'Nothing,' she snapped, inviting his curiosity even more keenly.

'I think there's something you want to tell me – would I be right?'

If she'd been less miserable she might have hesitated longer before speaking – or not have spoken at all. However, the details of Rose Stannix's letter came gushing out uncontrollably. She told him too, but in more vague terms, of the row with Ginny, leaving out what she herself had said about Hubert's demented revelation.

Tommy was furious and threatened to go right away to Stannix House and have it out with Rose. With great difficulty Lida persuaded him not to. If he had, her own treachery would have been exposed. He picked up his suitcase and turned towards Garravicleheen.

'If Hubert dares call up to our house, I'll tell him where to take his troubles.'

'It's not his fault!' Lida pleaded. 'Say you won't take it out on him.'

Right through the square and into Friary Street he

refused to answer her. By the time they'd reached the railway station near their house he'd calmed down.

'Yeah, you're right,' he admitted. 'No point in blaming him, he has enough problems as it is.'

She was almost relieved to breathe in the musty air of home. If her father had accepted Tommy's return without preconditions then surely he'd begun to relax his stranglehold over them all. Would he not learn from this compromise and, perhaps, see that he must compromise his futile dream also?

At the dinner table Josef showed no signs of having changed his mind. He ate silently and the dead weight of his sombre mood pressed down on them. The day had already brought more than its fair share of torment and Lida was driven to dropping her knife and fork in frustration on the oilcloth table cover.

'Talk to him, please,' she implored. 'He's your son and he came home. What more do you want him to do?'

Lowering the cup from his lips, her father rose and left the kitchen.

'Will you shut up, Lida,' Tommy whispered.

'I won't shut up. Someone has to say something.'

'Tell her to put a zip on it, will you, Mama?'

Anna Hendel rested her head in her hands.

'It's true someone has to say something,' she said, 'but there's a way to say it and a way not to say it, Lida.'

Her father was at the kitchen door again and whatever protest Lida might have made to her mother was muted by shock. In one hand he held the new tennis racket. In the other, the photograph. He placed them on the table but no one lifted their eyes.

'First I discover I can't be master of my own life,' he announced. 'Now I see I'm disregarded even in my own home.'

Taking the photograph and slipping it into his shirt

pocket Josef left them again. Lida, woken suddenly from the spell of gloom, rose to follow him but Tommy's hand was firm on her shoulder.

'You don't kick a man when he's down,' he said.

Anna was on her feet and steeling herself with a long, slow intake of breath.

'It's time your father and I talked,' she breathed and Lida knew by the resolute look on her face that it was best to let her mother take up the battle now.

For hours, she and Tommy sat in the darkening kitchen, both afraid to move, even to go and switch on the light or tidy away the dinner plates. The waves of conversation directly above gave them hope and brought despair in equal measure.

At ten o'clock, Lida remembered that Tommy was supposed to be rehearsing with The Silver Sound and whispered to him that he should go.

'I'll stay put,' he said. 'Things are bad enough as it is.'

Eventually, they both went quietly to their rooms. But not until dawn, until the first birds sang, did the house itself fall silent. Finally they slept, not knowing what that silence was made of.

CHAPTER 13

The acrid smell of vinegar invaded every pore of the Hendels' kitchen. A cold rain spat against the window and steamy tears wept down the inside. Boiling beetroots rose and fell in the big metal pot and little purple droplets splashed out to sizzle away on the hot range.

Lida and her mother busily sliced the first batch of beetroots and placed them in the row of washed jamjars on the table. Hands stained from the purple juice, they wiped away their perspiration with their bare arms. Pickling beetroot was not Lida's favourite pastime.

Try as she might to find out, she was, as yet, none the wiser as to what had passed between her parents during the long night. She hadn't asked directly but even her heaviest hints met with a casual dismissal and a warning to mind her fingers on the sharp knife. Having slept so little and woken to yet more rain, Lida's irritation grew by the minute.

Today, she would know who her semi-final opponent was to be. The only thing she was sure of was that it wouldn't be Ginny. Mrs Mackey wouldn't risk that – for Ginny's sake. Between the remaining two, Marnie Cread and Phil Bowles, there was little to choose. Either one could make life uncomfortable for the opposition.

From the radio, tuned to the Home Service of the BBC, the unruffled, public school voice of Max Robertson, the tennis commentator, eased through the clutter of her mis-givings. It was Ladies' Semi-Final day at Wimbledon. The American girls had taken all four semi-final places and now Mrs Dupont, last year's champion, was playing Louise Brough, whom she'd beaten in the 1947 Final.

The soft putter of racket, ball, racket, ball was as hypnotic as Robertson's velvet tones. Even the bursts of applause were not enough to wake the lightest of sleepers. And yet, a gentle undercurrent of excitement thrilled Lida's tired mind into imaginings. 'Miss Hendel to serve, sweeping back that dark fringe, lays the ball up and ...'

The front door knocker slammed insistently and seemed to shock the smooth flow of the commentator's words. Even as Lida went through the hallway the loud din went on unabated. She pulled open the door impatiently and stepped back in surprise.

'Sorry to trouble you,' Hubert Stannix apologised. 'Is Tommy about?'

The rain had flattened his mop of grey hair to a drab, stringy mess. His face, shot through with the panic in his eyes, belied the evenness of his words.

'Only Mr Kinsella told me he'd left and I wondered if he'd gone to Dublin or ...'

Transfixed by his distracted look, Lida was unable to answer.

'Who is it?' Anna asked from the steam-filled kitchen.

Still Lida stared dumbly at the bedraggled caller, unaware of her mother's approach.

'Yes?' Anna asked, stepping between them.

'Hubert Stannix,' he told her, 'a friend of Tommy's. Could I speak to him?'

'Tommy is not here,' she answered. 'He is in the town.'

'I see,' Hubert said with disappointment. 'Sorry to have ...'

He began to retreat along the path taking careful, apologetic backward steps. Anna, unsure as ever of her English, whispered at Lida to ask him in. She refused to listen to Lida's objections, telling her that the man was soaked to the skin and needed to dry off. Besides, she said, he was clearly in no state to drive that 'peculiar blue car'.

'Would you like to come in and wait for Tommy?' Lida asked reluctantly. 'He shouldn't be long.'

'I really shouldn't,' Hubert muttered, stumbling over one of the many cracks on the path.

'Come,' Anna said. 'You must.'

As if entering some no man's land in that terrible war still raging in his mind, he followed them into the house. Anna drew a chair back from the table for him and cleared away the brown paper bag of peelings and the plates of sliced beetroots they'd been working on.

The expression of warning on her face made it clear to Lida that she was to make an effort to talk to their guest. On the radio, the commentator was doing his best to lighten the tension with his praise of Louise Brough's victory over Mrs Dupont. The news added to Lida's discomfort. Last year's Wimbledon champion beaten. It felt like a bad omen for her own prospects.

'It's an awful day, isn't it,' Lida stated, beginning where all awkward conversations seem to – with the weather.

'I'm glad he's not gone to Dublin,' Hubert said, still bound up in his own thoughts.

'He's just gone to get something for Mama,' Lida told him, for no particular reason except to keep the conversation going.

'I feel I can confide in Tommy,' he went on, 'things I barely understand myself.'

It was impossible to talk to Hubert. No matter what she said, his answer veered off on some tangent known only to himself. After several minutes of wasted effort, Lida was glad to have her cup of tea to hide behind. At first, Hubert's hand shook so much and rattled the cup in its saucer so precariously that Anna watched in dread anticipation. This rich cream-coloured set of delph had been her wedding gift from her friend, Magda, her touchstone to that place that was still her home.

By and by, however, soothed by the magisterial voice which had now gone on to describe the second semi-final, Hubert began to control his trembling. Looking out over his raised cup he seemed, at last, to be aware of where he was and with whom. He tried some of Anna's fruit cake and washed it down luxuriously with the strong brown liquid.

'Great cup of tea,' he said, licking crumbs from the corner of his mouth. 'And what can I say about the cake. Did you bake it yourself?'

'Yes, thank you.' Anna shyly bowed her head.

Hubert relaxed into his chair, settling himself in for a long wait. What, Lida wondered, could be keeping Tommy so long? Her mother should have had more sense than to send him for more vinegar. He was, by now, probably sitting on one of the high stools at the new American Ice Parlour in Glenmorgan House swapping detective novels with Jimmy Tobin. Or talking about the pigs on *Animal Farm*.

'It's so nice to be in a house,' Hubert announced with a sudden, unexpected vehemence, 'where people are so kind and not afraid to speak to each other.'

Coming, as it did, after yet another hesitant interlude, the statement seemed quite nonsensical. Lida began to feel an unwanted resentment towards this representative of the Stannix family. Even if he didn't share their views on the Hendels, his visit was bound to have unwelcome consequences. Hubert's concentration appeared to falter again and he searched the middle distance longingly.

'Up at the House,' he began, 'there's a locked room. We used to call it "the study". Everything there is covered with white sheets, the writing desk, the piano, everything.'

Anna, though she couldn't quite make sense of what he was saying, looked at him sympathetically, realising the depth of his distress. Lida shifted uncomfortably in her chair, guessing that more revelations were to come – revelations she couldn't trust herself with.

'You shouldn't upset yourself, Mr Stannix,' she said, barely concealing a plea for him to stop before it was too late.

'Locked,' he continued. 'Everything hidden away. My brother's ghost locked in our hearts and we can't let him go free because of this … this bloody awful secret of ours.'

It was plain to see that he wanted to unburden himself. All she had to do was ask and the undiluted truth would come. She felt like a spy on the point of discovering the one great weakness in the defences of her enemy's forces.

'If Rose heard me speaking like this,' Hubert said, 'she'd have me consigned to a mental home. She's already warned me, you know.'

Lida thought she heard the grating squeak of the front gate. She hoped fervently that she had.

'It's a terrible price to pay,' Hubert murmured. 'My sanity for my brother's honour. Am I my brother's keeper? Should I be?'

His strange question was directed at Lida and carried such a weight of suffering that all thoughts of treachery were crushed in her. The front door opened, bringing with it a loud reminder of the pouring rain.

'He's home,' Lida said with great relief and her mother, too, breathed easy again.

His father's Homburg hat was a size too big for Tommy but he didn't mind. He'd pulled down the narrow sides and brim to make it more 'American'. He showed no surprise at seeing Hubert in the small kitchen. In fact, for a brief instant, he showed no emotion at all. Lida wondered if he might say something about Rose's letter and hoped, for everyone's sake, he wouldn't.

'How d'ye like the hat, Hubert?' he asked, breaking into a bad actor's charming smile.

'Very fetching,' Hubert laughed.

'*Wo ist der Essig*?' Anna asked curtly.

'The vinegar!' Tommy moaned. 'Cripes, I forgot to get it.'

'I'll go,' Lida offered, seizing the opportunity to escape. 'I have to go to the club to find out about the draw.'

They didn't notice Hubert's trembling had started up once more. Beads of sweat had formed where the drops of rain had only just dried out.

'I should be getting back,' he muttered and rose clumsily from his chair.

His elbow caught the edge of his saucer and sent both it and the cup crashing to the floor. All four of them stared at the shattered remains rocking to a slower and slower tinkle on the cheap linoleum. One look at Anna made it clear to Hubert that he'd destroyed something very precious.

'I'm sorry,' he stuttered slowly and painfully. 'I'm so desperately sorry.'

Anna smiled bravely and nodded with resignation. Turning to Tommy, Hubert raised his hands and cupped them into fists on his forehead.

'This is unforgivable, Tommy,' he cried. 'Unforgivable!'

'Mama doesn't mind,' Tommy said, looking at his mother. 'Not much.'

'It's not only the cup and saucer,' Hubert tried to explain. 'It's more ... the reason I broke them ... not that I meant to ... but the reason I panicked and knocked them over ... it's unforgivable.'

'Game to Miss Todd!' the radio voice announced, as if that mattered now.

Tommy brought the quaking wreck that was Hubert

Stannix to the door. Muttered apologies came punctuated by heavy-hearted sobs.

'*Ich bringe ihn nach Cormackstown,*' Tommy told his mother and Lida.

Hubert lurched away from Tommy, stared at him for a moment and just as suddenly grabbed Tommy's hand in his own.

'You see!' he exclaimed. 'Again ... it happened again ... this is what happened ... why I broke those beautiful things.'

Fear shaded Tommy's eyes and the vinegar-scented steam was an oppressive mist over Lida and Anna.

'It was because you spoke in German, Tommy,' Hubert said. 'I have no right, I know, to react like this. But it frightened me. Please forgive me, I have no right to say these things. If it was anyone else I wouldn't dare. But you'll understand, won't you?'

'I'll take you home,' Tommy said evenly.

In spite of her own discomfort with the German language, Lida was hurt to hear someone else express it. She was sorry she'd given in to her mother's insistence on giving Hubert shelter, and was glad to see him leave.

'What on earth was that all about?' her mother asked as the Delage pulled away with Tommy at the wheel and Hubert crouched like a wounded soldier in the passenger seat.

'Don't mind that fellow,' Lida said. 'He's mad as a hatter.'

For once she felt no reservations about her crude judgement of him. In spite of her mother's displeasure, she refused to retract.

'He is,' she repeated. 'And he's broken that lovely delph on you.'

Anna swept up the fragments indifferently and dropped them in the bag with the beetroot peelings.

'They're broken,' she said. 'And that's it. They're no longer of any use.'

'We might find something to match the set in Molloy's.'

'No,' Anna said and an aura of optimism radiated from her that seemed to suggest that if she ever did buy a replacement, it would be as part of an altogether new set.

Or at least that was what Lida wanted to believe.

'I don't know why you can't tell me straight out whether we're ever going to escape this rotten house.'

The big, sustained, reedy sound of organ music replaced the hushed world of Wimbledon on the radio. A tune, 'The White Cliffs of Dover', with its reminder of war and parting, brought Hubert's pain to Lida's mind again. She fought against the surge of guilt. Her words came with more force than she'd intended.

'What happened between you and Papa last night?'

Considering her answer, Anna leant on the sweeping brush and when she spoke it sounded too much like a riddle to satisfy Lida's frustration.

'How can I put it?' she wondered aloud. 'You know when two countries are fighting one another and every so often, when one side advances, the border between those countries changes? Well, last night the border changed, for once, a little in my ... in our direction.'

'I'll get the vinegar,' Lida said, giving up all hope of a direct answer.

Outside, the rain had petered out to a light, vaporous spattering. After only a few minutes of walking, the heavy overcoat Lida had thrown on left her so stiflingly warm that she had to take it off. It was annoying to know the sun was so close, ready with its golden light, if only these clouds, a little less dark now, would just separate and be gone.

Her eyes lowered, she went along Friary Street like a vagrant searching the footpath for pennies or cigarette butts. Her thoughts turned to tennis. To backhand volleys, lobs, to that habit of hers of racing to the net. So engrossed was she that, at first, she didn't hear her name being spoken.

'Lida! Well, Lida.'

On the far side of the road, Mags Campion stood at the door of the newspaper shop. Lida looked around to see if someone else might have called her. It had to be Mags.

'Well,' Lida said and stayed on her side of the street.

There was nothing in Mags's face to betray any ill-feeling toward Lida. On the contrary, she seemed more than anxious to appear friendly. Lida was puzzled.

'You're playing Marnie Cread in the semi,' Mags told her. 'I bet you'll beat her.'

'Maybe,' Lida said, stepping back warily. 'See you.'

'See you,' Mags said.

As Lida went on she felt Mags's penitent eyes fixed on her back. She wondered if something had happened between Mags and Ginny. She had no idea what such a development would mean for her in the continuing battle with Ginny but she couldn't help smiling and thinking that, perhaps, the borders in her war were moving too. Her mother's words hadn't been a riddle. Lida had simply been deflected from their true meaning by her anger.

Things were looking up. Things were, at last, really looking up.

CHAPTER 14

'Can't you hear him sneezing and coughing?' Anna asked in exasperation as she held out the breakfast tray which Lida was so reluctant to take.

'He can't be that bad.'

The idea of acting as a maid for Tommy annoyed her intensely. Even if the weather hadn't been so perfect and her desire to get to the tennis club so urgent, Lida would have objected.

'I'll take it myself then,' Anna said with a practised air of martyrdom, but Lida took a grip of the tray and almost swiped it away.

'Don't spill the tea.'

By the time she'd reached the landing and bundled in by Tommy's door, a pool of tea sent out little streamlets to the porridge bowl and the plate of brown bread. Serves him right, she thought, if he gets into trouble for spilling tea on the embroidered counterpane on the bed.

'Breakfast is served,' she announced drily. 'Would you like me to feed you while I'm at it?'

A pair of bloodshot eyes gazed sleepily at her and exploded suddenly into life when he sneezed.

'I'm dying,' he groaned. 'You're a miller.'

'Will I get the priest?'

'Cripes, Lida, can't you see I'm flattened,' Tommy said, struggling to raise himself into a sitting position.

Lida landed the tray on his lap and he swayed to hold
it from falling. Snatching open the curtains, she jerked the
window upwards and the fresh air that had been pressing
to get inside swept past her, sending shivers through
Tommy.

'Cripes,' he moaned, holding his hands over his eyes.
'You should have told me you were going to do that.'

'I'll put an ad in the *Tipperary Star* next time.'

However, in the light of day, she was more convinced
that his illness was real enough. She lowered the window
a little and sat on the sill. The air was less sickly now but
still unpleasant. This was something else about the house
that she disliked. Whenever someone was laid up in bed
here, the old walls seemed to give off a dreadful odour of
every sickness suffered there over the years. For weeks
afterwards, the smell would persist and leave her feeling
vaguely unwell.

'I felt it coming on after that night in the marquee,'
Tommy snuffled as he sipped the warming tea, 'and when
I went out to Cormackstown with Hubert yesterday, I put
the tin hat on it. We sat in the car for three hours talking. I
was shaking like a leaf. I should have had more sense.'

'No danger they'd ask you in out of the cold,' Lida
observed bitterly. Dipping into the porridge with some
reluctance, Tommy held his half-filled spoon aloft for
a moment and then placed it back in the bowl. He took
a last sip of tea, dumped the tray on the bedside table,
lay back and sank into the pillow. Lida could almost
feel the throbbing in his head.

'As a matter of fact,' he said, 'they did ask me in.'

'Who did?'

'Your friend Ginny,' he told her. 'She came out to the
gates and asked Hubert if he'd like to bring me inside to
talk. I tell you, I got a bit of a land, so I made an excuse
about having to get home.'

Lida could just imagine the pretence of pleasantness on that holier-than-thou face of Ginny's. She had obviously wanted to stop her uncle talking to Tommy in private. If they went inside, she could ensure that he didn't say anything he wasn't supposed to.

'I know you two don't hit it off,' he continued, 'but she seemed fine to me.'

'I can't believe you're saying this,' Lida exclaimed.

'All I'm saying is, this nonsense about "foreigners" and this vendetta against us Hendels, maybe it's just the mother. I know Hubert doesn't think like that and, to be honest, I don't think Ginny does either.'

To think that only days before she'd actually *missed* having this traitor around. Now he was taking sides against her, fooled like all the others by Ginny's charm. Why couldn't he see through that snow-white liar? The evidence was irrefutable and if he wasn't convinced by what she'd already told him, she'd hammer home the truth. She repeated now what Mags had said about the portrait of Hitler and how she'd called them 'gypsies' and 'tinkers'.

'And she told you Ginny said all this?' Tommy asked doubtfully.

'She didn't have to tell me,' Lida objected, 'Mags wouldn't invent things like that herself.'

'So she didn't say it was Ginny?'

'Not exactly but ... but she didn't deny it.'

'Then it might have been Ginny's mother?'

'But Ginny said things too,' Lida cried. 'She said ...what did she say ... oh, yeah! She said, "People like you," or "the likes of you people" ... or something ... . But I know what she meant.'

Tommy leaned over on his side as if trying to decide whether to draw himself up again.

'People often say things they don't mean when they're

fussed,' he said. 'I do it myself. So do you.'

The urgent banging on the front door below couldn't have come at a better time. Lida simply didn't want to consider the possibility of Ginny's innocence. A quick exit from Tommy's bedroom and his too-reasonable argument might stop her from having to think about it. She hurried to the bedroom door but heard her mother below, already speaking to the caller. When he heard the second voice, Tommy dropped back and pulled the covers up to his chin.

'It's Ger,' he whispered. 'Tell him I can't go to Clonmel tonight, will you?'

'Tell him yourself.'

'Please?' he asked. 'My head is splitting. I couldn't talk to him now.'

She grasped the door handle with a white-knuckled intensity and, slamming it behind her, said:

'If it was Ginny flippin' Stannix, you'd get up.'

Ger Kinsella stood at the front door fidgeting shyly with the hat in his hands. His face redder than ever, he looked humbly at Anna as if blaming himself for the fact that she couldn't quite understand what he was saying. It was with great relief that he smiled at seeing Lida descend the stairs, though her look was still frosty after her angry encounter.

'I was just looking for Tommy,' Ger said. 'We're in action down in Mick Delahunty country tonight. You never know, we might do him out of business.'

Mick Delahunty's was the most popular band around. The Silver Sound were never likely to displace him. Another dreamer, Lida thought, tired of the world of dreamers; though at least Ger's dreams harmed no one but himself. She couldn't help softening towards him.

'I'm sorry, Mr Kinsella,' she said as kindly as she could. 'Tommy won't be stirring out for a while.'

The effect of her words wasn't as overwhelming as she'd expected. Brushing some flecks of dust he'd only now noticed from his hat, he shook his head slowly from side to side.

'Well, sure it can't be helped,' he reasoned. 'We'll manage, but will you tell him we got the tennis club dance. A feather in the old caps, you know. We'll have to be right for that one.'

The tennis club dance was where the championship trophies were presented. It was the highlight of the social year for the members. A grand meal was laid on and there was dancing and lots of spot prizes. Last year, Tommy had brought her but only to receive her trophy. The juniors had to leave by half-past nine. Not one for dancing, Lida had no objection to this particular rule.

'He won't let me down, sure he won't?' Ger asked of Lida and she was touched by this gentle desperation. 'We're not half the band without him, you know.'

'He'll be fine in a few days,' she assured and he went away, pausing at the gate to offer a grateful smile.

She didn't go near Tommy's room for an hour and when she did she felt no better disposed towards him. Her mother wanted to know if he'd like more tea and Lida went to ask him only because it offered the chance to make him feel bad about Ger Kinsella.

'The poor man thinks the world of you,' she sniped, 'and you wouldn't even bother talking to him.'

'I would have, only I'm sick,' he said. 'What did he say?'

Lida noticed the book half-hidden under his pillow. His eyes were clearer and there was a definite hint of attentiveness in them as he watched her.

'He said they'd get on fine without you.'

She'd meant to goad him but he was merely relieved. He closed his eyes smugly and seemed more than happy not to be going to Clonmel. She wondered if he was beginning to change his mind about the music. If he really was, she'd know better when she told him of the tennis club dance, their first big engagement.

'Oh, really,' was all he had to say on hearing the news. He turned to face the wall and its dreary flower pattern, emptied long before of any colour it might ever have possessed.

The day was holding up well and it was good to be out of the house, with its obnoxious reminders of ancient sicknesses and the treacherous talk of her brother. She couldn't depend on Tommy any more than Ger Kinsella could. But who could she depend on? At the tennis club, Mags Campion was waiting with an answer to that question.

Mags sat alone on the pavilion steps as Lida approached and there was no avoiding her.

'Well, Lida.'

'Well, Mags.'

'Do you want a partner?'

Lida surveyed the few girls hanging about the court. It didn't seem like she had any choice but she wouldn't make it easy for Mags. What she feared most was being let down again. It had occurred to her too that Mags's efforts at friendship might be part of some devious plan of Ginny's.

'I suppose.'

'I'm sorry about what I said,' Mags burst out. 'If I hadn't gone out to that house I never would've said those things. Are you sorry too, Lida, are you?'

It was all too overwhelming for Lida. Her suspicions seemed unfounded in the light of this startling apology. At a loss for words, she hesitated but Mags flooded the silence with more tearful claims and denials.

'... and it's a madhouse out there,' she blubbered finally. 'They're all daft, every one of them.'

While Mags had talked back her tears, Lida had gathered herself. There was one thing only that she wanted to know. Nothing else mattered at this moment.

'Which of them mentioned the photograph of Hitler?' she demanded. 'And called us names?'

'Mrs Stannix,' Mags admitted. 'It was Mackey who told her. But Ginny is mad too. She said I only got friendly so's I could find out about her father. But everyone knows what happened to him. He was a war hero, wasn't he?'

It seems not, Lida told herself. But if not a war hero then what exactly had he been? What was it he'd done that had brought such great shame upon his family, a shame they strove so hard to cover up? Had he been a spy for the other side, or a deserter? Or was it simply something about the manner of his death, as Hubert had hinted, something far less glorious than the heroic death Rose Stannix told the world about? As for Mrs Mackey, nothing about that woman surprised Lida now.

Her mind was far from tennis as she mechanically exchanged shots with Mags. There was no doubt now that Ginny's life didn't match the perfection of that image people had of it. Living in a house with a disturbed uncle, a troubled ghost of a father, and a mother who would go to any lengths to preserve the family secret could not be easy. In such an atmosphere of secrecy and shame, no one would remain untouched.

'I forgot to tell you,' Mags cried just as Lida was about to serve. 'Ginny mightn't be playing in the championship any more.'

'What!'

'She hurt her ankle. That's what I heard, anyway.'

There was no injury, Lida was sure of that. Ginny was backing out because the truth about her father was slowly leaking out. Perhaps she suspected that Hubert had told Tommy everything, that Tommy had told Lida and Lida told anyone who wanted to listen. Now Ginny was afraid to face those who shortly before had looked on her as a kind of goddess, the daughter of a heroic god of war.

Ginny's departure from the championship should have been good news, but somehow it left Lida feeling deflated. If she won now, it wouldn't prove she was the best. That hallowed silver tab would never have the same sparkle as last year's. However, if Ginny refused to play there was nothing Lida could do about it. All she could do was concentrate on her own game and ensure that Marnie Cread didn't deprive her of a victory which, even if it was to be tarnished by Ginny's absence, would nonetheless keep her name where it belonged – on the Junior Singles Championship trophy.

Getting down to some real work on her game, she was delighted that Mags had improved so much. Little or no time was wasted running after wildly struck balls and Lida was able to play more forceful shots without upsetting the big girl. It proved to be a very useful exercise and her new racket stood up well to the test. Even as she played she realised she had Ginny to thank for the fact that, at last, she had a good sparring partner.

In the dressing room, she basked in the tired satisfaction of having made real progress and looked forward to three more days of practising with Mags before the match with Marnie Cread. It was time, it seemed, to clear the air with her friend.

'Mags, what I said about the frilly knickers ...'

'It doesn't matter about all that now,' Mags laughed. 'But we won't fight again, will we, Lida? Or if we do, we won't say things, bad things, will we?'

In the late afternoon, as they walked home, the wide town square seemed to Lida as beautiful as any Italian plaza she'd seen in films or magazines. The tired grey buildings were invigorated by the golden light reflected from their high windows. Even the two statues in the centre of the square seemed less coldly concrete, the passage of sunlight across their stony faces firing them with a spark of remembered humanity.

Mags and Lida parted in good spirits, their plans for the next few days arranged, the bitterness of the previous days put behind them. All along Friary Street, the railway bridge and Monastery Road, Lida passed on the unshaded side. But at Garravicleheen, with the sun already in decline, she was shaken from her reverie as harshly as from a sleeping dream.

At the front gate of the house Lida stood wondering if she'd only imagined the sounds or whether they were, in fact, coming from next door. The sibilant slide of metal blade on metal blade, the sudden snapping stop, the soft fall of leafy branches on to grass.

She edged around by the side of the house and peered through the scraggy privet hedge, into the neighbour's garden. There was no one in there. Turning the corner of the house she saw, at first, nothing. Even the noise had ceased. Then her father appeared, the sun highlighting the almost blonde streaks in his hair.

With his back to her, he was raised to his full height, his rolled-up sleeves revealing the strong muscles of his arms. In his hands, the garden clippers sheared through the ragged laurel hedge, re-shaping it. The glossy leaves poured down around him as he turned slowly to look at her. They stood twenty yards apart but she could see the minutest tremor at the corner of his mouth.

He was on the brink, the very precipice of laughter or tears. And Lida was too. Laughter and joy it would be if his interest in life had been rekindled. But what if this display meant instead that they were to be condemned to this house forever?

Josef Hendel went back to his labours with renewed purpose and his daughter was left without a further clue as to their future. Nor would that tight-lipped silence reveal its true intention for days to come.

CHAPTER 15

As she woke on the morning of the championship semi-final, Lida at first thought the silhouetted figure at the window was some leftover image from her dreams. It bore the shape of her father and she'd been dreaming of him every night since the unexplained return to the chores of the garden. Then he spoke.

'*Habe ich dich aufgewacht?*'

'No, I was already awake.'

Over his working clothes he wore a trenchcoat so she knew, without having to get up and open the curtains, that it wasn't a good day outside. At least there was no hiss of rain or rustling of leaves. In fact, the stillness was so complete that the world seemed emptied of all the troubled echoes of the past and all the insistent daily din of the present.

'Is it going to rain?' she asked quietly, so as not to disturb the exquisite feeling of rest and timelessness.

'I don't think so. But it's a cold one.'

He hadn't come to talk about the weather, that much was clear. He looked like he had something more important on his mind. Lida tried hard to quell the rising sense of expectation with a forced yawn.

'I wanted to say …' he began, all the while fiddling with the collar of his coat.

'Yes?'

'There are things I need to explain to you,' he said,

'things I know I should've explained to you long ago. I suppose I wanted to believe that you and Tommy were still children, that you wouldn't understand.'

The unexpected turn in the conversation wasn't what Lida had hoped for but she was nonetheless curious for all that.

'This business of speaking German ...' he said.

'I was being stupid.'

'No. I can understand why it might confuse you. I know that German means one thing to me and something very different to you, something very different to a lot of people, I suppose, after ... after all that's happened.'

He sat on the bed and she breathed in the heavy, almost rubbery scent of his trenchcoat.

'To me, German is the language of my grandparents, my mother, even my father, whom I should hate, I suppose, but can't. I think in German. I dream in German. And Hitler and his ... his people, they took everything I worked for. Why should I let him take even the words from my mouth?'

Very tentatively, the question that had bothered her for so long formed itself in Lida's mind. She hoped that asking it wouldn't distance him again.

'All those things the Nazis did in the war, Papa, was it because they were German?'

'It was because they were cowards. A cowardice that grew out of their fear and insecurity and, in the end, made bullies of them. But there have always been bullies and always will be. They're everywhere. What happened in Germany only proves what can happen when the bullies take over.'

'Are we German?' she wanted to know. 'Or what are we?'

'We're human beings who live in a divided world. But Lida, for a few years in Czechoslovakia, I saw what can be done when people work together. Czechs, Slovaks, Hungarians, Jews, Germans and more, we built one of the best economies in Europe. I loved, I believed in Czechoslovakia. Now I may never see it again.'

She urged him silently to continue, to bring himself to a decision on their future now that he had talked about the past with such finality.

When he went slowly towards the door, her heart sank.

'We'll talk again,' he said. 'I hope your match goes well. Don't think I'm not interested in how you get on, Lida, just because I ...'

Lida closed her eyes, wishing a sleep would come from which she might wake to find him there again, so that this whole encounter could turn out differently. Yet, while she hadn't got what she'd wanted, she felt she'd been given something to halt her descent into total despair. He had spoken freely with her, no longer regarding her as a stupid child. It was enough, or, at least, all that she needed for now to keep her spirit and determination from flagging as she faced the toughest hurdle yet on her march to the championship title.

Marnie Cread was a tall, unfriendly girl of sixteen, who was famous at the club for two reasons. She had the longest hair and she was the worst loser around – worse even than Lida. Her brown hair reached down to her waist and when she played she plaited it up into a serpent-like coil on top of her head. Everyone knew when she was in trouble in a match. The tight coil would loosen and she'd pull at it so angrily that her hair threatened to come out from the roots. When she lost, she would heap accusations of cheating and insults on her bewildered opponent. Lida wasn't afraid of Marnie's loudmouthed antics but there was no doubt that she was a tough competitor.

Marnie's glance settled on Lida as they passed each

other by in the pavilion. Lida faked a shuddering look of
terror in response.

'We'll see who has the last laugh,' Marnie snapped,
betraying her state of anxiety.

'Who's laughing?' Lida shrugged and went outside to
await Mrs Mackey's call to action.

As usual, the club secretary was fussing about excitedly.
She checked the net and stamped down divots in the grass
court with the big flat-heeled shoes that seemed much too
large for her feet. In her hand she held a sheaf of papers
on which she ticked off her endless list of items to be
attended to. Lida couldn't summon up any hate or anger
towards her. All she felt was the familiar longing to escape
from her miserable house.

When the Stannix family car edged to a halt at the gate
outside, Mrs Mackey's efforts intensified. So, Ginny was
to play after all, Lida thought, with more relief than
trepidation. She felt quite relaxed and watched the club
secretary's frenzied preparations with a wry smile. It
seemed everything had to be just right for the arrival of
these honoured guests. However, Lida didn't feel any of
the old resentment and as the curious scene developed at
the blue car, a wave of sympathy enveloped her.

Ginny, it soon became apparent, didn't want to leave
the back seat of the car. As the attention of the twenty or
so spectators turned towards the spectacle, it was impossible for them to hear what was being said, though Rose
Stannix had, by now, opened the passenger door.

Mrs Mackey, disturbed by the sudden hush around her,
looked up from her papers. She raised her hand to wave
at the occupants of the car but lowered it quickly when she
realised something was amiss.

The rustle of Rose Stannix's black crinoline dress
drowned out her insistent words. Though quite a small
and beautiful woman, she had a fierceness, a kind of manic

energy, that was palpable even at this distance. Hers was the kind of beauty that needed no decoration. Her hair, almost as fair as Ginny's, hung in careless, unbrushed waves and yet didn't seem at all wild or unmanageable. Her face, small and perfectly formed, was almost repellent, so fearsome did it seem.

Now she was jerking open the back door and Lida could see quite clearly the look of horrified embarrassment on Ginny's face. In the driver's seat, Hubert stared straight ahead and drummed out a patient rhythm on the steering wheel.

'You will play!' Rose shrieked.

Among the crowd, eyebrows were raised and muted exclamations exchanged.

'Rose,' Hubert said, and turned to speak more quietly to Ginny, his words lost as the audience strained to hear.

Lida felt like an intruder and imagined this same knot of onlookers gathered around her own home, listening to the door-banging and arguing of her family. She considered their open-mouthed expressions with disgust and hurried inside to the empty pavilion. Her agitation grew as she paced up and down the corridor between the dressing rooms.

She wished she'd never mentioned Hubert's half-revelation to Ginny.

She was almost tempted to go and tell the girl that she hadn't spread any gossip about her father's death but Mags's breathless arrival put the thought to the back of her mind.

'I didn't get up till half-twelve,' Mags gasped, 'and then Mammy wouldn't let me out till I finished my dinner.'

She leaned back against the timber wall to catch her breath.

'There's blue murder going on out there,' she continued. 'Ginny doesn't want to get out of the car. What's wrong with her, I wonder?'

Lida shrugged, feigning disinterest. She needed something upon which to take out her pangs of guilt. The rackets in her hand were as good a set of scapegoats as any.

'I wish I had a decent racket,' she said though she knew this one had served her well of late.

'You have a new one!'

'Oh, I don't know. I just can't get used to it.'

'Hey,' Mags said. 'You're just a bit nervous, that's all. The racket is fine.'

It felt good to have Mags back on her side. Especially now, when she felt she didn't deserve friendship.

'At least I'll have someone shouting for me,' she said. 'That'll make a change.'

'You might be surprised,' Mags told her. 'I heard a few people saying they hoped you'd win the championship.'

'But they all despise me. I know they do.'

'You're so touchy, Lida,' Mags grinned. 'Someone only has to look crooked at you and you get right thick.'

'Mags!'

'It's true though. But you're changing. You're not as wild as before.'

The backhanded compliment didn't please Lida. She was beginning to wonder whether she'd done the right thing by making up with Mags. However, she managed to contain her anger which, she suddenly realised, might be proof of what her friend was trying to say.

'I don't mean wild exactly,' Mags said, searching fruitlessly for the right expression. 'Anyway, no one expects you to be perfect. Perfect people are a right pain. Like Ginny. That's what they're saying now.'

So, the tide of popularity, Lida thought, was turning in her favour. Not long before, she had wanted it to, had wanted Ginny to be seen for what she was. Or what Lida had imagined she was – a spoiled, devious brat. Now, however, the change held few pleasures for Lida. The longing for vengeance it might once have satisfied was now all but gone.

And what did it mean, in any case, to be liked by everyone? Did it necessarily make you a better person? And how long would such popularity last? As long as it had lasted for Ginny? Until the next heroine came along?

Around the corner of the pavilion door, Mrs Mackey's hawk-like head cocked itself haughtily. She peered at Mags with a heavy frown to show her disapproval of her choice of friends.

'We're waiting for you, Miss Hendel,' she barked. 'You're disrupting my schedule.'

They followed her outside with Mags awkwardly imitating the woman's snappy little steps. Mrs Mackey looked up at the sky as if warning it not to dare spill so much as a drop. Ginny sat between her mother and uncle at the bench near the pavilion steps. Rose Stannix held her daughter's hand in an unbreakable grip.

The laughter on Lida's face melted to an unintended but unavoidable look of apology. Ginny looked through her, not so much ignoring her as bound up in her own pain. By the time Lida had reached her end of the court and turned to face the menacing spectre of Marnie Cread, she was entirely unsettled. Right through the warm-up she stumbled and fumbled her way around the court, feeling the perspiration rise on her forehead as soon as she began, despite the coolness of the day.

Making no impression on Marnie's first service, Lida proceeded to lose her own, through a series of unforced errors. Double faults, lame second service shots bouncing up magnetically to Marnie's crushing forehand. Games flitted by her in an unstoppable rush. In all she succeeded in winning only two of her own service games.

During the eighth game, the score at 5–2, Lida's new

racket flew from her grasp as she stretched to a wide shot. Down on her hand and knees, riveted by Marnie's callous grin, she was about to utter a loud German curse but somehow held back.

Instead, she remembered Mags's words about her having changed. She almost laughed to herself at the thought. The only change was that she was being demolished more completely than a total beginner might have been.

'Lida! Miss Hendel,' Mrs Mackey cried, 'would you please continue. We don't have all day.'

Her tone of voice made it clear that she regarded the next match, Ginny's, as more important than this miserable affair. The barely concealed insult spurred Lida on to take two points in succession but it was more luck than skill that caused the ball to stay inside the line. She was still a long way from getting past Marnie's blockbuster style. An idea would form in Lida's mind to spin the next shot or lob it, but the ball was returned so quickly that the only thing she could do was make a hopeful swing.

Finally, like most of the previous ones, this game too slipped away from her.

The disastrous first set was over. Six–2. A rout. Lida sidled over to the bench where a worried Mags sat holding her towel.

'I thought you were gone home,' she told Mags cattily.

'I was roaring. Did you not hear me?'

Lida buried her face in the towel and tried to focus her mind on her game, tried to recall the lost points and find the reason for her pathetic display. All she saw was her father, poised with his shears in the garden; Hubert, humming in his 'Swinging Tree'; her silent mother slicing beetroots; and Ginny, firm in the grasp of Rose Stannix. All their disappointed faces seemed either to blame Lida or plead with her to help, she couldn't decide which. But her own strength had been sapped, she was powerless. She could neither protest against their blaming nor conjure up any answer to their silent pleas.

'Can you help me, Mags?' she asked, emerging from her temporary hideaway. 'Can you tell me what I'm doing wrong?'

Mags's heavy lips moved but, much as she wanted to, there was nothing she could do or say. Lida pressed the towel to her eyes and, at once, felt a hand on her shoulder. It wasn't Mags. She looked sharply behind her and saw Hubert Stannix leaning in over the back of the bench.

'Tell me to mind my own business if you like ...' he began.

She was too surprised to tell him anything.

'... but I think I can point you in the right direction.'

The situation was too desperate to ignore advice, wherever it came from. Even if it came from a man who climbed trees to sing nursery rhymes.

'She's a tall girl and she doesn't like bending low,' he said. 'In fact, if I'm not mistaken, her back is giving her some trouble. So, keep the ball down and push it on to her backhand. That way it's even harder for her to reach. All right?'

'Thanks, Mr Stannix.'

'Hubert,' he said. 'And you don't have to thank me. I'm simply returning a favour.'

As Lida made her way to the opposite end of the court, she heard Rose berate Hubert in a strangled whisper.

'Really,' Rose Stannix fumed, 'I'd have thought you'd learned your lesson about mixing with those people.'

Lida was ready for Marnie Cread now. Between them the older Stannixes had given her the incentive she needed to fight on.

Hubert had offered a solution to breaking Marnie's grip on the match. His sister-in-law had fuelled the fire of her indignation. It proved to be an unbeatable combination.

The snake-like coil atop Marnie's head was soon sliding forward perilously. She stooped low to scoop ball after ball but the best she could do was touch it away beyond the line with the timber edge of her racket. Mrs Mackey did her utmost for this grocer's daughter but was given few opportunities to work her wiles.

Now Mags's encouraging cheers rang in Lida's ears as did the applause from Hubert and a few others when she struck yet another telling ace service. The match ended to Marnie's frenzied protestations and a louder than expected gust of approval from the gallery. At the net, Lida offered her hand to her opponent.

'You took advantage of my bad back,' Marnie cried but Lida's mind was elsewhere.

It had just occurred to her that Marnie Cread coped very well with being a bully without having to be at all German. Lida's mind was clear enough too to see that for most of the game, except that moment when it had slipped from her hand, the racket had caused her no problems. The elation she felt had less to do with her victory than with the feeling of reassurance these thoughts brought her.

'D'ye hear me,' Marnie raged. 'You made me bend so much I can hardly walk.'

'Maybe you shouldn't have played today, Marnie,' Lida replied calmly, looking wide-eyed and innocent, 'when your back was so bad.'

Marnie cast Lida's hand aside and stormed away to the pavilion. Before Lida had reached Mags, Mrs Mackey had waylaid her.

'Really, Lida, there's no call for that kind of talk,' she complained. 'Tennis is a social game. You'd do well to rem-ember that.'

'But, Mrs Mackey,' Lida said evenly, 'I have to win that trophy again. It looks so well on the mantelpiece. Under the picture of Adolf Hitler.'

Mrs Mackey held on to the net as she paled and mouthed little animal-like sounds.

'I feel sorry for you,' Lida said, 'I really do.'

She joined Mags at the bench nearby as the club secretary muttered something about Ginny trouncing her in the final.

However, Ginny's performance in the match against Phil Bowles was not one to inspire fear. She struggled even more unconvincingly than Lida had done. All her former grace and calm seemed, by degrees, to desert her.

Unlike Lida, she did manage to win the first set but it was more to do with Phil's nerves than any good play on her part. In the second, Ginny's confidence took blow after blow until it collapsed completely. When she spoke quietly to Hubert after the set it seemed likely that she wouldn't be continuing. Mrs Mackey waited with a look of benign patience as Hubert talked his niece back on court. Whatever it was he said helped to steady her play just about enough to see her through to winning.

The tense burst of applause led by Mrs Mackey and Rose Stannix, and taken up only briefly by the crowd, did nothing to soothe Ginny's temper. To her mother's dismay, Ginny refused the hand proffered to her by the club secretary. Mrs Mackey was so shocked that her raised hand seemed rigidly locked into position for minutes after. Sitting on the bench, Lida and Mags heard every word of the ensuing argument.

'You're coming with us,' Rose Stannix told her daughter, 'after you've apologised to Mrs Mackey.'

Ginny's mask of defiance threatened to slip at any moment and Lida found herself willing the girl to hold her ground.

'I'm walking home,' Ginny said, 'and I'm not apologising to anybody.'

Though she had no reason to, since she'd come to the

club dressed for action, she went towards the pavilion and climbed the few well-worn steps. Her mother made to follow her but Hubert stood in her path.

'Let her be,' he said. 'She'll be fine.'

'I certainly will not. She's disgraced us with her common behaviour.'

'No one's been disgraced, Rose,' he answered, and turning to the club secretary, added, 'I'm sure Mrs Mackey understands and will be gracious enough to accept my apology on Ginny's behalf.'

Flushed with delight at being addressed so courteously, Mrs Mackey broke into a servile giggle.

'Of course,' she enthused. 'Why, yes, of course, Mr Stannix.'

Hubert took his sister-in-law's arm and while he didn't quite have to drag her from the place, he did have to keep a tight grip on her as they went. By now, Ginny had gone inside the pavilion and though there were others who needed to go in there, for one reason or another, nobody was prepared to make a move in that direction. No one except Lida.

'I'd better go and get changed,' she told Mags. 'Will you come?'

Mags was more than reluctant to face Ginny and Lida could understand why. Their brief friendship had, no doubt, ended in as bitter an exchange as Lida's had with Mags. Lida herself wasn't too happy about going inside but the breeze blowing against her sweat-soaked blouse was sending shivers through her, shivers that felt strangely like a thrill of expectation.

'I won't be long so,' she said. 'Make sure you wait for me.'

The boards of the pavilion floor creaked noisily with every step and every creak echoed ominously through the frail building. Ginny wasn't in the corridor so Lida wasn't surprised when she opened the dressing room door and found her there. Lida didn't know whether she should greet the girl but Ginny kept her head down so she decided not to.

She slipped off her tennis shoes and the damp socks and went behind the small partition to change into her dress and cardigan. She listened for the trace of a sob or some telltale sniffling, but there was none.

When she emerged, the warmth of her cardigan already spreading along her arms and back, she saw that Ginny had lowered her head even further. The short gold-blonde hair had fallen forward and Ginny's fingers threaded themselves through the wayward strands. Lida got one fresh sock on and, realising it was inside out, went on regardless with the second, such was her hurry. The buckles of her shoes refused to co-operate for a minute or two until she finally managed to secure them, grabbed her rackets and rushed to the door.

'He told you everything, didn't he?' Ginny said, her head gripped between her hands.

The door was open. There was nothing to stop Lida from leaving and she could think of plenty of reasons to go. Another unpleasant war of words was likely to start up between them. And could she trust herself to leave Hubert and Ginny's father out of it? The last thing she needed was another of those snide letters from Rose Stannix, letters that would surely arrive whatever the outcome. But none of these doubts were enough to outweigh the look of genuine hurt on Ginny's face when, at last, she rose and faced Lida.

'Look, Ginny ...' Lida said, 'I shouldn't have repeated what he told us but it was only a hint ... a vague hint. He didn't explain it. Not to me, anyway.'

'He told your brother. He said that getting it off his chest had made a new man of him. But what good is that to me?'

Ginny's breath came in despairing gasps.

'God, I'm so tired of all these lies,' she whispered. 'All this hatred for people we don't even know. And secrets, grubby little secrets. I'm sick of hiding them.'

Lida sat down beside the girl she would soon be facing in the championship final. She knew all about hatred, had hated this girl before she'd ever set eyes on her and hated her even more when she'd met her. And all that hate had come from the same place as all hate – fear. In her case, the fear of losing her title. And, all the time, they had more in common than either could have imagined.

'*Die geheimnisse Versammlerin*,' Lida said, the words springing unbidden from her memory.

Ginny's distress turned to puzzlement.

'It's a nickname I gave myself once,' Lida explained. 'It means someone who hoards secrets.'

'You have secrets too?'

'Doesn't everyone?'

'Do you have someone to share yours with?' Ginny wondered.

'No.'

So few words had passed between them and yet they seemed somehow to have been drawn so close that it was impossible to imagine any distance separating them again.

'My father ...' Ginny said and paused to prepare herself for the hungry truth begging to be spoken.

CHAPTER 16

Another game had begun out on the main court and in the Pit behind the pavilion. The sounds of life returning to normality were a reassuring background to Ginny's story. It was as if the truth, so plainly spoken, had shocked the world into a new vitality.

'My father didn't die in France. There was no village, no sniper fire, and Hubert wasn't there with him at the end. All of that was invented by my mother because she couldn't accept what really happened.'

Those first words burst forth from Ginny in a heaving rush but now she'd begun, she sat up straight and leaned her back against the wall, the hard part over, the stone rolled back from the icy tomb. Her hands no longer gripping the seat, the long fingers worked slowly about each other as she went on.

'He was in London, on leave from the Front. But it was only to be for a week and there wasn't time to come to Ireland. He stayed in Kensington with some cousins of ours and one night he borrowed their car to go and meet his friends from the regiment. He'd been drinking a lot. Hubert says they all had. It was the only way they could forget the terrible things they'd seen, the terrible things they had to do to survive.'

Lida, feeling quite helpless, hoped that listening would be enough. There was nothing else she could think to do.

'On his way back to Kensington, he crashed. No one knows exactly how or why. It was a straight stretch of road but he lost control of the car and was killed instantly.' Her face betrayed no emotion and Lida wondered if it was because the girl had lost all feeling for her father.

'My mother didn't even give herself time to cry before she started changing the story. As soon as Hubert brought my father's body home, she persuaded him to help her, as she put it, to protect the family name. Hubert was a captain too – he'd been decorated for bravery. She convinced him to have his initial on the medal changed to "R", for Robert, my father. That would be the final proof, you see, that he was a hero after all.'

From the corridor came the familiar echo of Mrs Mackey's busy little stride. Ginny fell silent as the door squeaked open and the dressing room was filled with the club secretary's strident tones.

'Are you all right, Miss Stannix?' she asked, but she was glaring at Lida. 'I hope no one's upsetting you in here.'

Ginny eyed her so malevolently that Lida decided she'd better speak before the tenuous peace of the dressing room was shattered.

'We're just having a chat,' she said, 'a private chat.'

Working her wrinkles into an offended frown, Mrs Mackey looked from one to the other, not at all pleased with this unexpected union. She withdrew huffily, breaking her own golden rule about slamming doors in the pavilion. Ginny began again as if the interruption had never happened.

'That's why she hates all of you so much. Like Hubert says, there has to be somebody to blame and anyone she regards as a "foreigner" will do.'

Lida motioned to Ginny to stop talking and, reaching across to the handle, pulled the door open. As she suspected, Mrs Mackey stood there, crouched, her large flat ear cocked.

'I … I seem to have lost my fountain pen,' she stuttered. 'Can you see it, Lida? It's terribly valuable, you know.'

'It's sticking out of your pocket.'

'So it is,' Mrs Mackey cried, scrambling to her feet. 'So it is.'

Her obsequious smile failed miserably to hide her shame and fury. As she pottered away, Lida could almost hear that spiteful mind searching for something to say. But Lida was too quick for her. Mrs Mackey turned sharply, a look of triumph on her face.

'*Auf wiedersehn*,' Lida suddenly said with a smile, and the woman's eyes lit up wildly.

'What's that you said?'

'*Auf wiedersehn, Frau Mackey.*'

All she'd said was 'Goodbye', but as far as Mrs Mackey was concerned she might have been calling her an old bat.

Mrs Mackey broke her door-banging rule again and the timber structure swayed beneath Lida's feet. She went back into the dressing room, making sure the club secretary heard the door bang shut with an echoing finality.

'Such an awful woman,' Ginny said. 'I wonder if she'll be so nice to us when we have to sell Stannix House.'

Lida couldn't honestly say she'd been shocked by what she'd heard up to now. Hubert's strange talk had prepared her for all of that. This last statement, however, left her flabbergasted.

'Sell Stannix House?'

'Maybe it was more than just pride that made Mother invent her story. She wanted a perfect husband to remember but he was never what you would call perfect. Not that it matters to me. He was kind and generous, too generous, maybe, and I loved him even though I knew he was hopeless at business affairs and all that. What I didn't know, and what my mother pretended not to know, was that he was a gambler. When he died there were huge debts. She tried her best to pay them off, but it looks like we have to sell the house now and there'll be no more boarding school for me. That's about the only good thing about this whole mess.'

She looked at Lida, a sudden urgency in her eyes.

'I don't want you to think I hate him,' she said. 'I don't. I never expected him to be perfect and losing the house means nothing to me. I could never be happy there.'

'So you'll be leaving town?'

'Hubert is insisting we stay,' Ginny said. 'He thinks there's no point in us moving away. He says we have to face up to the new realities. You know, I can't believe how much he's changed since he met Tommy. He's started to take charge of things like never before and all that aimless wandering and climbing the Swinging Tree and everything is over. You saw him there, didn't you?'

Lida shrugged unconvincingly, remembering quite well the words she and her mother had heard him singing from his high perch.

'My father and Hubert played in that tree, the Swinging Tree, when they were young. There was this long branch about five or six feet from the ground they'd swing out of and jump into the grass below. Ever since he came home, Hubert went there every day, in every weather. It was so sad. He was like a little boy who couldn't understand why his brother never came to play any more.'

Ginny paused as if to consider this stark image of loneliness. It was time, Lida knew, to tell her how much they had in common. The cloud over the family's happiness; the loved, imperfect father; the clinging to a past that became less real as time went on. When she'd finished, she felt that for the first time someone had understood the confused background to her own difficult present.

She felt drawn to Ginny in a way she knew she could never have felt with Mags. Not that she blamed Mags for this. It was just that her and Ginny's experiences were so alike. Mags, she realised, had problems too but of a different nature, dealing with the taunts and the self-consciousness over her size. Lida wouldn't be casting her aside now just because she had a new friend, that much she was sure of.

'I hate to ask you this, Lida,' Ginny continued in some trepidation, 'but there is a favour you could do me and I won't mind if you feel you can't.'

A cheer rose from the main court and they both looked out by the small dressing room window as if to avoid briefly what was about to follow.

'It came to me just now. Maybe I'm mad but now that Hubert and I have ... well, come this far, maybe there's something we can do to shake Mother from this lie she's living. Hardly even a lie any more, because I think she truly believes that story of hers now.'

'What can I do?' Lida asked, troubled by a vision of the beautiful but somehow sinister face of Rose Stannix.

'If you and Tommy came to the House to visit, it might make her see that you're not monsters. At least she'd have to accept that we don't think like she does and that she can't make us hate when we don't want to.'

Difficult as such a confrontation promised to be, Lida couldn't refuse. Her slowness in reacting, however, left Ginny feeling uncertain.

'I know it's a lot to ask,' she said, 'especially after that letter she wrote to you.'

'You knew about that?' Lida bristled.

'She wouldn't listen to reason. I begged her not to do it but she was so frightened that Hubert had told you about all this, she couldn't be stopped.'

'It's all right,' Lida said, 'I'll do it but I can't promise Tommy will come. He's stubborn – even more stubborn than I am!'

They listened for a while to the laughing, excited sounds

from outside. Lida was sure that the talking was over, which added to her puzzlement at Ginny's next question.

'What does your mother call your father?'

'Josef,' Lida answered. 'She just calls him Josef, I suppose.'

'Mother calls my father "The Captain",' Ginny confessed. 'She always used to call him Bobby but now it's "The Captain". And she talks about him like he's still there. Hubert has to plant roses along the side wall because, as she says, "The Captain" likes roses. She can't say he *liked* roses. She can't accept that he's gone.'

'Maybe it's better not to think of him as being gone,' Lida said, trying to imagine how she would speak of her own father in the same circumstances.

'But we have to let him go free, let him escape from that locked-up study. We all have to let go.'

If Mrs Mackey had been eavesdropping now, she would certainly have thought Ginny quite as distracted as her young, grey-haired uncle. But given all that had gone before, Lida knew better.

'When should we come?'

'Tomorrow,' Ginny urged. 'Would you come tomorrow?'

'Fine,' Lida said, realising that it was no time for hesitancy and wondering what it was she was letting herself, and perhaps Tommy, in for.

'The secret-gatherer,' Ginny mused. '*Die* ... what was it?'

'*Die geheimnisse Versammlerin.*'

'It sounds so beautiful. Maybe you'll teach me some German when all this is over. Will you?'

'*Natürlich,*' Lida said, savouring the word, the language of generations of Hendels. 'Of course I will.'

CHAPTER 17

'Go to Stannix House?' Tommy cried. 'You must be joking.'

Her brother's recovery had been remarkable. Too remarkable. He'd used her to get out of last night's performance with The Silver Sound. And now he was refusing, after all her torturous explanations, to return the favour.

'You're a selfish lout, Tommy Hendel,' Lida told him. 'You fooled me into getting rid of Ger and now ...'

'I was sick.'

'You were in your back. You're just trying to wangle your way out of the band 'cause you can't put up with the hardship.'

Tommy threw his book angrily on the bed but when he looked at her, his eyes betrayed him. The anger was a front for confusion.

'That's not true,' he said weakly.

'So where's your accordion? How come you don't practise any more?'

'It's up at Ger's. I forgot to bring it home.'

'You did. I'm sure,' Lida sneered but, sensing his discomfort, she desisted. 'Do it for Hubert, will you? He thinks the world of you, Tommy.'

Tommy stretched back on the faded coverlet of the bed. Though his feet hung out over the end, so tall was he, to Lida he seemed like a boy who'd grown up too fast.

'All right,' he sighed, his mind elsewhere, 'I'll go. But if that woman says one word about Germans and all that stuff, I … I won't take it lying down.'

Lida thought it best not to argue the point, happy to have his agreement. There was plenty of time to persuade him not to overreact if Ginny's mother turned sour. Before she'd reached the bottom of the stairs Lida's delight was already overshadowed by more unpleasant thoughts.

Here she was, plotting and scheming with Ginny to undermine Rose Stannix's obsession with an unreal past. If the plan worked, the Stannix family could return to a life of normality. Yet, at the same time, the Hendels continued to endure an equally damaging obsession. She had waited for her father to say more to her now that he had made the first attempt to explain himself but nothing had happened.

He was in the garden again, burning the dead leaves and branches in a rusty barrel. The sharp tang of smoke filtered into the kitchen where her mother sat, listening to radio music and dreamily peeling potatoes for dinner. Her air of sweet unconcern had its usual maddening effect on Lida.

'Why is he doing all this work, Mama?' she asked. 'Why doesn't he explain?'

'Lida, try to be patient …'

Anna continued with her peeling, seemingly unperturbed, the rhythm of her work as one with the sway of the music.

'He's happy out there,' she said. 'Let him be.'

Retreating from the window, Lida came to her mother's side. She wanted to take the knife from her hand and do to the radio what her father had done. But *she* would make a proper job of it, root out the music forever, that stupid romantic music that fools you into believing that all is right with the world.

'When he's happy, we're supposed to be happy,' she

said. 'And when he's miserable, which is most of the time, we're supposed to be miserable too. Is that it?'

She hadn't heard him approach the back door and as it swung open she was sure he'd heard what she'd said, but was past caring. When she saw his bright smile, however, she knew she'd been wrong.

'I hear you won your match,' he beamed. 'Well done.'

It would have been easy to submit quietly to his praise, to pretend that this was all that a daughter should expect. But she refused to allow herself to. A suggestion of Ginny's she had rejected at the time came to mind.

As they'd walked home together, her new friend had wondered aloud if her mother's story might move Lida's father to see the error of his ways. Lida had objected that even if she started to tell him, he wouldn't give her a chance to finish, he'd be so angry.

Now the details of Rose Stannix's fantasy spilled from her lips before she'd even made up her mind to tell it. She spoke with such quiet force that Josef's reaction wasn't as she'd predicted. He offered no protest, could find no words to express his feelings. But they showed, too visibly.

'Living in the past.' The phrase ran funereally through her wandering, disconnected speech. With each repetition of it, the transformation of his rugged cheerfulness to the dark, familiar lines of dangerous intent became more stomach-wrenchingly awesome. He stared at her as if she'd betrayed him to some fearsome enemy. In a final twist of the knife she told him of Mrs Mackey's deceitful lie about the portrait of Hitler.

Anna stood up from the table and wiped her hands on the tea towel by the bowl of steeping potatoes. She placed herself before him and he stepped back, stumbling blindly against the kitchen dresser.

'It's time, Josef,' she said.

He backed away further as if her new-found intent was

a pistol pointed in his direction. The handle of the door to the hallway refused to fill his searching hand. Tommy was on the other side now, trying to get in. When he managed to force the door open, his father brushed him aside and lurched out of the kitchen.

'No,' Josef Hendel said. 'No. I'll decide when it's time. I'll decide if it's time. I ...'

The cracks in the ceiling widened and narrowed with his comings and goings in the room above them. Lida sat heavily into a chair, thinking she would never reach him now. Whatever tenuous bridge had been strung together between them had crashed into the broiling waves of his embittered soul. The prospect of going to Stannix House, though it hardly mattered now, seemed likely to prove as futile as trying to change her father had been.

When he left the house by the front door they were almost relieved that he was gone. The cracking and breaking of branches in the garden was the last thing they expected to hear. As one, they moved to the back window and were shocked by what they saw.

Josef rushed maniacally from one pile of clippings to the barrel and on to the next pile. His face smeared with black ashes, he seemed to them like some primitive man, absorbed in a strange ritual of burning. Flames burst from the barrel. Shooting, snapping sparks rained down on him in a hellish eruption. They feared for his safety, for his very sanity, but could not move.

A sudden breeze swept a thick blast of filthy grey smoke at him. For a second or two, Josef was lost from sight. When the smoke lifted, he was on his knees, his hands clasped to his streaming eyes.

Anna slid past Tommy and Lida and in an instant was outside, lifting her husband with all her strength. He didn't want to get up, they could see that. But she was too strong for him. He stood, at last, tall above her, his head bowed. Her hands grasped his waist and his, very slowly, held her and then held her closer. Tommy put his arm over Lida's shoulder and she let it rest there.

Time was elsewhere. There was no knowing how long they stood there clinging to each other. Anna and Josef, Tommy and Lida. The Hendels. And then the spell was broken.

Josef lowered his gnarled fingers from his wife's back. Looking towards the house, he gestured to his children to join them. At first unwilling, Lida was persuaded by Tommy's encouraging glance. Gathered awkwardly around the barrel, they waited for Josef to speak. But it was his actions that spoke first.

He stooped down to gather a few more wizened stalks and threw them in the barrel. A small, tired flame sputtered into life. From his pocket he took the old photograph of the farmhouse in Moravia and the aged, yellowing deeds. He dropped them into the rusty, ashen depths and the flame was shot through with a last flickering dance of colours. The dark smoke cleansed itself to a whisper of white and their eyes followed its flight, above the high laurel hedge to the evening sky and beyond.

'Tomorrow,' he said, 'I sign the papers for the new factory house, No. 2, Slievebawn.'

It was Anna's idea, despite the fact that dusk had fallen, to go and look the new house over. The large, echoing rooms seemed impossibly bright for the time of evening. Upstairs, her mother showed Lida the room that was to be hers. The view across green fields to the distant Devil's Bit, a mountain which seemed to have a bite taken from its peak, was delightful. Only when she'd been staring out by the window for a while did a question arise in her mind.

'How do you know so much about the house?' she asked. 'You never told me you came over here.'

'It's best to be prepared,' Anna smiled, 'for whatever might happen.'

'You knew all along we'd be getting a new house, didn't you?'

'No,' Anna insisted. 'But I never gave up hope.'

In the next room Lida found Tommy looking out at the curious landmark that was quickly fading from view as an evening mist gathered over the fields. His earlier enthusiasm had dissolved and he seemed quite downcast.

'What's wrong?' she asked. 'Don't you like it?'

'It's grand.'

'Why are you so grumpy then?'

Moving a small block of discarded timber around the floor with his foot Tommy hunched his broad shoulders.

'I don't know. It's just … as soon as we get our own home, it's time for me to move on.'

'You don't have to go, Tommy,' she said. 'Papa won't stop you playing music. Things will be different now.'

'One way or the other I'll have to go,' he continued. 'If I stick with the music, there's no point hanging around this town, I'll get nowhere. I'll end up like Ger Kinsella. And if I go to university, if I get enough honours, it still means going away.'

'But this will always be your home, no matter what you do.'

He kicked away the block of timber and stood tall again.

'We can't expect perfect endings,' he said. 'I read that in one of Hubert's books. "No perfect endings, only new beginnings. The courage to start all over again and the imagination to dream new dreams." Good, isn't it?'

'Did one of the pigs on *Animal Farm* say that too?' Lida joked but as they looked out at the mist hanging like a low cloud over the fields, she repeated Tommy's words to herself like a prayer.

Heading back to Garravicleheen, Tommy and his

mother walked ahead of Lida and her father. 'Well, what
do you think of No. 2, Slievebawn then?' Josef asked after
a while.

'It's beautiful,' Lida said. 'I can see the Devil's Bit from
my room.'

Her hopes for the following day's visit to Stannix House
were raised once more. Ginny had contributed, though she
wasn't to know that yet, to the events of the past few hours.
One truth, the unravelling of the legend of Captain Robert
Stannix, repeated at Ginny's suggestion by Lida, had
helped Josef Hendel to face another equally painful truth.
Now Lida wanted Ginny to share such a moment with
Rose.

'By the way,' Josef asked, 'that new racket of yours, is it
all right? I can always get you a better one, if you like.'

'No, the racket is ...' she began but she had no use for
that impossible word, 'perfect', any more. 'It's fine ...
really, it's fine.'

CHAPTER 18

Stannix House was a mere half mile from Garravicleheen but on that Saturday afternoon in July, their every step was weighed down with such dread it seemed to take forever to get there. Tommy and Lida had little to say to each other. Along the narrow country road, nature itself was subdued and, above them, the trees were empty of bird life. Or the birds had nothing to sing of in the heavy, insipid air.

At the high-pillared gate they paused before being sucked in along the lane tunnelling its way through the tangle of foliage. The light at the other end of the meandering lane seemed even greyer than it had out on the Cormackstown Road. Before them, the shoddily elegant red-bricked house gaped with its big window-eyes. The front door stood open, but the hallway was black as pitch as they approached.

Passing by the tennis court on the front lawn, Lida saw that the net wilted forlornly and the grass was in need of cutting. At the open door she thought about calling Ginny's name but noticed a rusting chainlink bell-pull hanging there and grasped it too tightly. The sound of the bell volleying through the hallway sent her reeling back. To her consternation, the bell-pull came away in her hand.

Tommy blushed a bright pink and threw his eyes up to heaven.

'You flippin' eejit,' he whispered in exasperation, 'I

knew we shouldn't have come here.'

At last, the house stirred from its torpor. From the top floor came the thudding of hurried steps. Further back along the hallway there was a sudden clattering of kitchen sounds.

'Cripes,' Tommy cried, ducking in beside Lida at the threshold.

The chain tinkled uncontrollably in her hand and she turned on Tommy angrily.

'Will you stop hopping around like a frog.'

'She's above peeping out the window at us,' Tommy explained. 'Mrs Stannix. You should see the face of her. Let's clear out.'

'You're not going anywhere,' she told him firmly.

'I'm telling you, she'll have our guts for garters.'

A stream of light filled the hallway as a door opened at the far end. Hubert Stannix walked confidently towards them but it wasn't the Hubert Stannix they knew. The shock of wavy grey hair had been fashioned to a tidy, scalp-hugging neatness. He wore a black, smartly cut dinner suit and a carefully balanced black bowtie beneath the crisp white collar of an impeccable shirt. As he offered his hand to both of them, a pristine shirt cuff fell languidly over his wrist.

'So good of you to come,' he said. 'Ginny's fixing a tray for us.'

Both speechless, they followed Hubert through the wide hallway, passing by a grand, carpeted staircase. He reached for the shining brass handle of a large double door and, hesitating for a moment, looked back at his guests.

'The study,' he said and with a flourish flung the door wide.

There were no ghostly white sheets covering the furniture now and no musty air of neglect, only the gleam and the waxy odour of polished timber and the golden glow of yellow flames in the black marble fireplace. Yet, there was something uninviting about the scene and Lida couldn't bring herself to follow Hubert and Tommy through the open door.

The broken chain she held behind her back provided an excuse to delay her entrance. She held it out to Hubert.

'I ... I broke this,' she said, 'it just came off in my hand. I'm sorry.'

'Not the first time that thing came apart,' he smiled. 'No point in trying to fix it now, I suppose. Well? Aren't you coming in?'

He dropped the chain into his pocket and guided Lida inside. She tried not to let him feel her tremor of unreasonable fear. She didn't believe in ghosts, but the barely audible knocking noises from somewhere above sent her heart racing so that it was easy to imagine a disturbed presence still lingered here.

The room had all the hushed dignity of a museum. Bookshelves on either side of the fireplace were crammed with ancient tomes; a glass-domed clock on the mantelpiece, with its precise mechanics visible, spun out the slow seconds; silver-framed photographs stood on every available surface, portraying the dead generations of Stannixes.

And on the piano, the wry grin of an army officer was captured for eternity inside the largest frame of all. A clipped moustache above the slightly parted lips, the peak of his hat casting a light shadow over the strong forehead and the pale, questioning eyes. She had never seen him before but there was no mistaking who he was. The similarity with Ginny was striking. Captain Robert Stannix, soldier of misfortune.

'Bobby,' Hubert said, and Lida felt like she'd been prying where she shouldn't have been. 'If he was here now we wouldn't all be so quiet. I mean ... Bobby was the life and soul of the party.'

He stared into the fire and Tommy and Lida looked at each other imploringly. Their messages were the same: 'Please, say something, please.'

'Isn't it bad news,' Tommy muttered, 'when you have to light a fire in July.'

The brass poker in Hubert's hand, like everything else in this room, seemed too valuable, too full of ancient significance, to actually use. When he plunged it in among the blackened turf, Lida half expected it to crumble to dust.

'Bobby always had to have a fire going in here,' Hubert mused, 'even on the warmest of days. He said it made him feel at home, somehow.'

The clinking of teacups from the other side of the door was a welcome relief. Hubert rose from the hearth, his vigorous smile reasserting itself. He placed the poker back in its matching bracket, went, a little too urgently, to the door and almost collided with Ginny as she swept inside with the silver tray. The eyes of all four fell on a dangerously teetering cup near the tray's outer edge. Ginny, swaying back and then briskly forward, managed to keep it from crashing to the polished, bareboard floor.

'Damn nerves,' Hubert said. 'All shot to pieces.'

'We're all nervous,' Ginny reassured him and turned to Lida. 'Sorry I took so long. I'm not very good in the kitchen, I'm afraid. Thanks for coming.'

Ginny's bright crimson dress seemed to light up the sombre room and her busy presence soon took their minds from the real purpose of their visit. Tea was poured, sugar and milk dispensed and cucumber sandwiches arranged on plates in a flurry of good-humoured banter.

'Three spoons of sugar!' Ginny exclaimed to Tommy's embarrassment. 'I might as well pour your tea into the sugar bowl.'

They sat around the fireplace and soon Hubert was talking animatedly of his plans for their future. He already had a buyer for the house but wasn't saying who. He'd made a bid on one which Lida knew quite well on Castle Avenue which was very close to her own new home in Slievebawn. There was no hint of regret in his voice, nor were there any telltale signs on Ginny's face.

The announcement that he'd found himself a job left Ginny as happily bemused as it did Tommy and Lida.

'Colonel Trant out in Dovea has taken me on as an estate manager,' he explained. 'I start Monday week.'

The conversation faltered briefly from time to time but Lida busied it along with her own good news about the impending move to Slievebawn and how Ginny had played her part in it. Soon they would not only be friends but near neighbours, and the prospect pleased all of them.

An hour had passed before the dull thudding from upstairs became too insistent to ignore. Lida could almost imagine Rose Stannix up there beating her fists in despair against the walls. It even occurred to her that they might have locked Rose into her room, but she dismissed the thought as soon as she looked at Hubert and Ginny. They would never do such a thing. Unlocking rooms was what they were about. Now, however, their new resolve was being tested to its fragile limits.

Ginny was becoming frightened and her unspoken panic infected all of them. A moment of truth had been reached and their fragmented words fell away, leaving a palpable void. To their surprise, it was Hubert who stepped into the breach.

'Would you do us the honour,' he asked Tommy, 'of playing something on the piano? It's dreadfully out of tune, no doubt, but we'd really appreciate it.'

The heat of the fire had washed all of their faces with a high, red glow. Tommy, however, was positively violet with anguish and doubt at Hubert's overly polite request.

'Cripes,' he objected. 'She'll have a canary if ...'

'Tommy!' Lida cried, shocked at his loose talk.

'It's quite understandable,' Hubert said. 'I shouldn't have asked. Just having you here is marvellous. But you know me. I do get a little carried away.'

There was too much of the old Hubert in his self-pitying eyes. The fear distorting Ginny's good looks too had Lida on edge. She was about to turn a pleading look on Tommy but he'd already stood up and was moving towards the piano.

'I'm a bit out of touch,' he said, 'but I'll give it a shot.'

In spite of Tommy's headstart, Hubert was at the piano before him fumbling so inexpertly with the lid that it half-opened and dropped onto his fingers. He didn't appear to notice.

'If you can play it half as well as you play the accordion, we're in for a treat.'

Had she not felt so grateful, Lida might well have been annoyed at her brother. His uncertainty was replaced by a cocky casualness as he sat on the piano stool and turned out a rolling stream of arpeggios, nodding to himself with satisfaction.

'It's not so bad,' he told Hubert. 'I've played on worse.'

Neither of them noticed, as Lida and Ginny did, that the noises from above had come to an abrupt halt. Lida did her best to produce a comforting smile and Ginny tried hard to match it.

'What would you like hear?'

'Anything,' Hubert enthused. 'Anything at all. Something lively maybe. We may even dance, what do you think, Ginny?'

Tommy teased out a few more rising octaves, loosening up the stiff keys as he thought of what he might play. He raised his fingers an inch above the keyboard and counted.

'A one, a two, a one two three four.'

With great gusto, he pounded out a swinging bass and

a wonderfully tense snatch of mid-range melodics. A sweet sensation of promise filled the hungry spaces all around, a promise that the music would rise and rise to a crashing crescendo.

'"In the Mood",' Tommy declared above the chopping chords.

'Good old Glenn Miller,' Hubert cried. 'Ginny, will you dance with an old flat-footed codger?'

Encouraged by Lida's repeated pleas, Ginny rose and Hubert snatched her out on to the centre of the floor. Hubert was far from flat-footed. He danced with ease, rocking back and forth to the brilliantly sustained rhythm of Tommy's playing. Lida, in her delight, had to admit to herself that her brother was good at this.

She'd only rarely heard him play the piano since they didn't have one at Garravicleheen. It was no surprise to her now that Ger Kinsella wanted him in his band so badly. Nor was it any surprise that making music was what Tommy wanted to do with his life. As she listened, she was almost persuaded to tell him not to give up so easily because of one bad night in a marquee tent. But the notion was forgotten as she was prevailed upon to take Ginny's place beside Hubert on the floor.

She'd never danced in her life, except in front of the mirror in her bedroom. Her heavy-leaded stumbling might have been insufferable to her had it not been for the light-hearted atmosphere. Still, she was glad to let Ginny take the floor again to follow expertly her uncle's every move. Finally, Hubert began to complain cheerfully of tired legs and collapsed in satisfaction into a large Victorian sofa by the bay window.

It was Ginny's turn now to drag Lida to her feet, insisting that she learn the steps of the fox-trot. Toes were trodden, knees bumped together and chairs collided with but, in time, Lida found herself mastering the once mysterious art of dancing.

As they swayed together to the beat, Lida wondered how she was going to face her new friend in the championship final. Hatred was no longer the clear motive it had once been to beat Ginny. In fact, when she thought about it, she didn't really want to beat Ginny at all, afraid that she might upset the delicate peace of mind Ginny had achieved with her help – afraid too that their friendship might end as soon as it had begun.

When they'd eventually danced themselves to a standstill, Lida was sure the visit was at an end. A keen sense of unfulfilled promise hung in the air, as if all the carefree jollyness of the afternoon had been a waste of time and effort. The renewed, but somehow less ill-tempered, noises upstairs seemed to confirm their worst fears.

'You'll play us one last tune, Tommy,' Hubert asked, 'won't you?'

'Sure,' Tommy said, but he was clearly anxious to leave.

'He's played quite enough, Uncle Hubert,' Ginny said. 'Be fair now.'

Lida had the distinct impression that Ginny knew what her uncle had in mind. She was sure she hadn't mistaken the undercurrent of panic in the girl's plea. Hubert, on the other hand, looked suddenly determined.

'Do you know "These Foolish Things"?' he asked Tommy.

Her eyes closed tight, Ginny turned from him and leaned forward, balanced tremulously on the edge of her chair. Lida expected her to spring at any moment to her feet but instead she rocked back and forth slowly and quietly. At the piano, Tommy gaped helplessly about him, wondering what he should do next. Lida's blank stare offered no clue.

'That was their song,' Hubert explained, 'their party piece. Bobby at the piano and Rose ... she had a wonderful voice. You have no idea how ... how different she was then. Will you play it, Tommy?'

'Ginny?' Tommy asked.

She nodded her agreement but her eyes remained shut. Hubert went to the door and opened it a fraction. He tamed the black butterfly of his dickiebow which had gone askew during the dancing. Clearing his throat with a dry, petrified cough he looked to Tommy.

'When you're ready,' he said.

Tommy's introduction was subdued but the bittersweet strains of the tune needed no emphasis. The light tenor of Hubert's voice eased itself casually into the broad, sad spaces of the haunting musical landscape.

'*A cigarette that bears some lipstick traces,*
An airline ticket to romantic places,
A photograph or two,
These foolish things remind me of you ...'

On the upper floor, a door flew open and Tommy's fingers slipped the keys into a brief discord. The descending footsteps banged out an alternate and opposing beat to that of his playing. Hubert stared fixedly out by the bay window as if willing himself to continue, despite the nervous, stuttering flow of notes from the piano.

'*The winds of March that make my heart a dancer,*
A telephone that rings but who's to answer,
Oh, how the ghost of you clings,
These foolish things remind me of you.'

The door moved wearily on its hinges. The music faded away, giving out altogether on a glaringly off-key note. Rose Stannix stood in a long silk dressing gown of autumnal colours. The deep rusty reds, the dusty browns, the ochre yellows of fallen leaves. All eyes were instinctively drawn to her, even Ginny's. Rose, however, seemed oblivious of their presence.

She raised her arms towards Hubert in readiness for

dance. He drew her inside from the cold hallway and gave Tommy the signal to continue. Rather stiffly at first, Tommy searched through the range of keys to find the lost tune. There was no stiffness in Rose and Hubert's gliding movements. Silken was the word that came to Lida's mind, as silky smooth as the dressing gown Rose wore. And her words when they came were silken too.

'He was a wonderful, foolish man, my Bobby, wasn't he?' she said to no one in particular.

In their slow circuit of the floor they had reached the door again. Rose withdrew her hands gracefully from her brother-in-law, acknowledged Tommy's efforts with a barely perceptible raising of her eyebrows and left them to consider the silence.

What, if anything, had been achieved? Lida wondered. There had been no malicious outburst towards Tommy and herself, leading to reconciliation; no thunderous argument with Hubert and Ginny and no tearfully accepting outcome; no admission of her lies or that the past was over and done with. And yet, Hubert seemed more than happy with himself. He answered their querying looks with enthusiasm.

'Bobby,' he said. 'You heard her say Bobby, didn't you? Not the god-awful Captain.'

'She said he was a foolish man,' Ginny muttered, deeply offended.

'Was!' he repeated. 'Was! She spoke about him in the past tense, don't you see? And she meant foolish in the best possible way, Ginny.'

As Lida and Tommy made to leave, Hubert's optimism had begun to sound hollow. The sense that he was clutching at straws was overwhelming. Lida was reminded of a night some months past, when she'd gone to the Stella Cinema with Mags. She couldn't remember what the film had been now but the last reel had been mislaid and the lights had gone up to a chorus of boos. They'd been given their money back but never got to see how the film ended. The same feeling of frustration bothered Lida now.

'Listen,' Hubert said, as they trudged out along the driveway. 'I'll be cutting the grass on the tennis court here this evening. Maybe you'd like to come and practise with Ginny some afternoon.'

Besides the fact that she had no desire to return to Stannix House, in spite of her new friendship, it didn't seem like a very good idea to spend the week before a final practising with your opponent. Her doubts weren't easily hidden.

'Hubert, really,' Ginny cried and told Lida, 'Don't mind him. I understand.'

Lida wished the bend in the lane was nearer so she could disappear from sight and not have to see Ginny's downcast face. She glanced at Tommy but he stared as blankly as Lida had done earlier when he'd looked to her for help.

'Thanks a lot for coming,' Ginny called and Lida knew that if she turned to look, she'd find it impossible to refuse Hubert's invitation.

Then she thought of something that might make her visit a little less intimidating. Something that would ensure that Rose's wrath, if it came, wouldn't descend on Lida alone.

'I'll be out around three tomorrow,' she called. 'Would it be all right if Mags came?'

'Of course,' Ginny said without hesitation.

Once they'd rounded the bend Tommy shook his head and said: 'I'm not saying anything about the Stannixes now but that house gives me the heebie-jeebies. I wouldn't go back in there if I was paid. You must be daft. Daft as a brush.'

CHAPTER 19

There had been too many awkward moments on that first visit of Lida and Mags to Stannix House. Mags had only agreed to come when Lida convinced her that she needed to have her there on her side. However, to Lida's embarrassment, Mags had attempted a befuddled explanation of her part in the row with Ginny. Ginny had been as gracious as ever in taking her share of the blame, but the whole business had left a sour taste in all their mouths.

'There's no need to say you're sorry, Mags,' she said when Ginny had gone inside to get some drinks for them. 'It isn't the time.'

'I'm sorry ...' Mags began and when they'd realised what she'd just said, they both laughed.

No need to say you're sorry. The words etched themselves in Lida's mind and she began to realise what she'd expected of this visit. It was ridiculous, of course, but she'd imagined Rose transformed from her tense, fearful self to a pleasant and charming woman, full of regrets for her former spitefulness. So regretful, in fact, that she would have done anything to make up for what had happened between them. But Rose hadn't even shown her face and it seemed that little had changed.

However, as the days passed, in that week before the championship final when their visits to Stannix House became daily, Lida sensed a slight, but very definite, lightening of the atmosphere. Nothing was said, no heart-rending confessions were blurted out, no emotion-filled scene of reconciliation occurred. It was more like a slow tide coming in along a vast sandy shore with a lone figure walking uncertainly towards the advancing waters.

On that first day Lida and Mags had stayed outside on the front lawn all afternoon, never venturing near the house itself. The next day, they went around the back of the house and sat in sunchairs listening through the open french windows to the Wimbledon Ladies' Final on the radio. Last year's beaten semi-finalist – the tall, blonde American, Louise Brough – was the winner, but Lida wasn't bothered about such omens any more.

Come the third day, they were sitting just inside the same French windows when they heard the tinkle of glasses on a tray outside the drawing room door. Ginny waited for a few minutes before easing the door back. All three of them seemed to see the silver tray with its three glasses of lemonade at the same time and each one registered the same catching of breath. Ginny's face was positively glowing as she brought the tray inside.

It had been difficult for Lida to summon up the will to beat Ginny in the final before this. Now, as she watched her coming so close to escaping the hell of the past, it seemed altogether impossible to inflict unhappiness on her. As she and Mags emerged from the gateway of Stannix House that evening, the problem was very much on Lida's mind.

From around a bend in the road, the distinctive blue Delage appeared with Hubert at the wheel. Mags linked her friend's arm and Lida could feel her shaking as she muttered, 'I hope to God he doesn't stop and talk to us.'

Which is precisely what he did. Mags cringed and tried to hide herself behind the smaller girl. She wasn't having much success either in hiding her astonishment at the change in Hubert – from a wild-eyed, bushy-haired recluse to this suave, smartly dressed man-about-town.

'How is the practice going?' Hubert called above the burr of the car engine.

'Grand,' Lida said.

'You're looking forward to the big one then?'

'Not really,' she responded, surprised at her unplanned honesty.

Mags took her eyes off Hubert for long enough to show her own surprise. At the turn of the key, the noise of the motor puttered out and the busy, natural sounds of the narrow country road imposed themselves.

'Why ever not?' Hubert asked.

'I don't know,' Lida responded, 'I just wish I was playing someone else in the final.'

'I see,' he nodded. 'I know exactly how you feel.'

His smile had turned a little more wistful and he was remembering something. A memory that brought with it some mixed feelings, it was clear.

'You know,' he began, 'I played Bobby in our school final once. He was the favourite but I knew his game so well, you see, I knew that if things worked out for me and maybe, well, not quite so well for him, that I could do it. And I did. But, you know, the hardest part was willing myself to beat him.'

He chuckled to himself and it might have been an eerie echo of his mad, empty years if not for his slow, relaxed stretching back into the car seat.

'I actually cried when I got the trophy – I was fifteen! I told him I didn't beat him because I hated him or anything and that I'd just been lucky. He told me I'd won because I'd worked hard and I'd made my own luck. That was just like Bobby. A great one for talking sense when it came to just about everyone but himself. He was a fool, like Rose said, but a happy, glorious fool, Lida.'

The strangest feeling overcame Lida. It seemed to her

that the spirit of Captain Robert Stannix was at last free and that through Hubert, he'd given her this message, as a gift of his gratitude. And she knew he would repay the others too, Ginny and Rose. Somehow, she was certain that her next call to Stannix House would show that the foaming tide and the solitary walker would have advanced within a very few paces of each other.

Next day, when the three girls had entered the drawing room after another afternoon on the front lawn tennis court, Rose Stannix was waiting for them. She gestured briefly to the lemonade and home-made biscuits laid out on the large round table, allowed her lips to curl down at the edges and left.

Lida could see that like Hubert, Rose had returned to a kind of normality. No longer was she wearing the autumnal dressing gown. Instead, she was dressed in a soft, greeny-blue tweed suit. The pale blue polo-neck jumper she wore emphasised her pearl-white neck and matched the powdery blue of the delicate veins there. Her hair, set in loose, springy waves, was kept in place with an equally pale blue hair-band that might have looked foolish on any other woman.

It didn't matter to Lida that she'd kept her distance. What mattered was that she was clearly drawing closer to a realisation of the truth of her life – and her husband's. Ginny radiated optimism.

During those first two days of practise at Stannix House it was clear that Ginny's mind wasn't on the forthcoming match. She seemed to lack enthusiasm and the signs of disinterest, though small in themselves, were obvious to Lida. That occasional giving in when a shot passed just beyond her reach. A hint of hesitation from time to time as she prepared to serve. These things seemed to mirror her preoccupation with more vital concerns. The will to win was absent.

Ginny's attitude began to change with Rose's first tentative advance on the drawing room. Lida knew immediately that the spark of determination had been rekindled and what surprised her was how that determination showed itself.

At first, she was sure that the fair-haired girl was simply making fun of the grunts and groans, the constant mutters of self-admonition that had once marked her own play. By now, self-control had become second nature to Lida, helped by the fact that she hadn't wanted to attract Rose's attention. The feeling was always there that Rose was watching every move on her front lawn.

It soon became clear that Ginny wasn't out to tease. She'd taken on Lida's style and Lida, reminded of her own mirror-image not long before, wasn't impressed.

'You're picking up my bad habits!' she called, only half in jest.

'I've been a goody-goody long enough,' Ginny said.

'Mrs Mackey will blame me for the new Ginny,' Lida replied.

'Just let her try.'

They matched each other, serve for serve, shot for shot. There was so little between them that Lida knew one lucky or unlucky bounce of the ball could decide matters in the final. But even that stroke of luck would come only after a lot of hard work. In her own way, Lida realised how her father must have felt after his years of working and saving when History took such an unlucky turn for him.

At times in those final days before the match, she wondered whether it was worthwhile even bothering to train if, in the end, it all hinged on something beyond her control. The wrong tuft of grass, perhaps, in the wrong place.

Hubert's words about making your own luck helped only a little. It was her father's new lease of busy life that

really kept Lida going. The simple fact that he'd begun all
over again after his disappointment proved to her that no
defeat need ever be final.

Giving up wasn't in her nature, any more than it was in
her father's. It had taken a long time to recover from his
set-back, but that was understandable given the huge
dimensions of his loss. Her own loss – if it came and she
was determined that it wouldn't – would be very small in
comparison and she would quickly get over it. And at
fourteen, she still had three more chances of winning that
junior title back.

So engrossed was she in her preparations that she took
little notice of the drama unfolding between Tommy and
Ger Kinsella during that week.

Each day, without fail, Ger had called to the house in
growing desperation as the night of the tennis club dance
approached. Tommy had avoided him at every turn until
finally, at dinner time on the Saturday of the championship final, the matter came to a head.

Sick with nerves, Lida couldn't eat. She watched the
clock count the seconds with a deliberate slowness, caring
nothing for her sense of urgency.

When the knock came to the front door she was glad of
the distraction. Thinking it might be Mags, she rushed out
by the hallway only to find Ger, hat in hand, hunched in
an attitude of pleading.

'Is he in, by any chance?' he asked.

She was in no mood for making excuses for her brother.

'I'll get him for you,' she said. 'Will you come in?'

'No, you're in the middle of dinner. It's no time to be
calling but I had to see him.'

When she reached the kitchen, Lida fixed Tommy with
such an ill-tempered glare that he knew, without her having to speak, who was at the door. He grimaced and
pressed his fingers into his forehead.

'Cripes, Lida,' he whispered, 'you didn't tell him I was here, did you?'

'He's waiting,' she said and sat down with an exquisite sigh of malicious satisfaction.

'Mama?' Tommy pleaded.

Anna shook her head. She wasn't going to let him hide behind her this time. Josef looked from his wife to Tommy to Lida.

'What's all this about?' he wanted to know.

'Tommy doesn't want to play in the band any more,' Lida explained, 'but he's afraid to tell Mr Kinsella.'

'I'm not afraid to tell him,' Tommy objected, 'I just don't like having to.'

Josef looked out by the half-open kitchen door and saw Ger pacing up and down the footpath outside.

'Tell him now, Tommy,' he said evenly. 'Don't leave the man waiting.'

Tommy pushed back his chair and got up. But instead of going to the door he retreated to the far side of the kitchen. Lida, her apprehension over the afternoon's prospects at fever pitch, lost her patience.

'Don't be such a coward,' she said. 'Go out and face him!'

'It's not that simple,' Tommy said. 'See, I told him I'd play for the tennis club dance and ...'

His father's brow wrinkled in displeasure.

'... and,' Tommy went on, 'I only said it 'cause I felt sorry for him. I didn't really mean it.'

On his feet, Josef went and closed out the kitchen door quietly. He turned to Tommy.

'You made a promise,' he said. 'You must keep it.'

'But you're the one who wanted me to pack in the music,' Tommy exclaimed. 'Now you're telling me to play. I don't understand.'

'I don't want you to stop because of me.'

'I'm not stopping because of you,' Tommy said. 'I haven't even decided if I'm giving it up yet.'

'I can see that,' Josef told him. 'But, in the meantime, you must keep your promise. A man is only as good as his word. Whatever you decide to do with your life, the same rule applies.'

His panic given way to astonishment, Tommy walked around the table and headed into the hallway. Lida's mind was suddenly far from tennis as she realised how momentous an event this was.

'Whatever you decide to do with your life,' her father had said. Only days before, the words might have been an admission of defeat for Josef. Now, however, his declaration fitted like the last piece of the once impossibly difficult jigsaw that was the Hendel family life.

As Tommy and Ger spoke together outside, Lida's attention wandered lazily back to the clock. Half-past two, it announced. She bounced up from her chair and in a dizzy flurry told her parents she had to go. Racing upstairs, she foraged in the wardrobe for her whites and a fresh towel, flinging them over her shoulder in a heap on her rackets. There was no sign of her runners and she rushed back down to the kitchen where her mother held them up, freshly whitened and criss-crossed with new laces.

'Thanks,' she said, grabbed the runners, dashed out the door and realising her hasty word of gratitude wasn't adequate, looked back in and added, 'Thanks very much.'

Josef and Anna laughed as her head disappeared from view in a flash and she was pounding up the stairs again. She grabbed the bundle from the bed and descended with a last call into the kitchen. Her father came into the hall to meet her as she reached the end of the stairway.

'What time are you on?'

'Four,' she said, brushing past Tommy and Ger at the front door.

'I'll be there,' he called.

Lida stopped at the gate and wheeled around.

'But you have to work after dinner, don't you?'

'I'm taking a few hours off,' he said. 'It's a big day.'

'I hope I don't let you down.'

'Do your best, Lida,' he told her, 'and you'll never let me down.'

My best, she thought, my best. Good enough for Papa, but would it be good enough to win the championship? Good enough to engrave her name on that precious silver tab?

CHAPTER 20

'Miss Stannix. Miss Hendel,' Mrs Mackey called. 'Come to the net, please.'

The club secretary was becoming impatient with the two girls who seemed to her to be in league together, disrupting her meticulously planned programme for the day's events. This was her third call to them. They had been warming up for ten minutes and, as she checked her watch once again, they showed no signs of desisting.

'Really,' she muttered, still unwilling to voice her disapproval of a Stannix family member too loudly, and more than a little afraid to provoke Lida now that her lie had been uncovered.

The club grounds were thronged and along all four sides of the main court there was no gap for the latecomers to squeeze into. Tommy stood near the net with his mother, biting his nails and talking in whispers, but Anna was too nervous to listen.

In their privileged position on the bench near the pavilion steps, Hubert and Rose sat, and between them no words passed. Lida's father hadn't yet turned up and this was one of the reasons for the girls' complicity in delaying the match. Lida tried not to blame him and instead thought about how taken aback he would be when he looked over the heads of the gathering and saw what had caused such a panic in the dressing room twenty minutes before.

They hadn't been able to speak as they prepared themselves for the task ahead. Smiling at each other's fumbling attempts to get the right runner on the right foot and knot up rebellious laces, they swung from attempts at meaningless pleasantries to finding themselves tongue-tied again.

Only when they'd been fully rigged out and had sat on opposite seats for a few quiet minutes did Ginny break the silence with a bemused air.

'Lida?' she asked, 'where's your new racket?'

Lida looked slowly along the bench and then peered underneath. Only the old racket was to be seen.

'Ginny,' Lida cried, 'stop messing. You're hiding it, aren't you?'

But she was speaking more in hope than anything else. They both searched the dressing room from top to bottom and went out into the corridor and beyond to the club grounds but, even as they did so, Lida guessed what had happened. She'd left it on the bed in her hurry to leave. Mags, who'd joined in the search, volunteered to run up to Garrivcleheen to fetch the racket but Lida was already wondering if this was meant to be. She and her father were friends again and refusing to use the old racket, even if he was never to know of this crisis, seemed like a rejection of all he'd done for her.

'No, Mags,' she said, 'I'm going to use this. Papa is coming today and I think I should.'

Ginny looked at her doubtfully.

'You could use one of mine,' she said, offering the Blue Flash that had wreaked such havoc against Mags.

'No, and I'm not trying to be petty like before,' Lida explained. 'I just feel this is the right thing to do.'

As Ginny strolled towards the net and Lida came to join her, they hid the mounting strain behind casual smiles. They shook hands across the net and Lida, despite her disappointment at her father's continuing absence, managed a joke.

'May the best man win,' she said.

'Excuse me!' Ginny laughed and the murmurs of the crowd raised themselves a decibel or two to an excited hum. 'This is a game for ladies. No hard shots now, do you hear?'

The club secretary eyed the blonde girl suspiciously but, in the end, refused to believe the lovely Ginny was capable of sarcasm.

'Quite right, Miss Stannix,' she pouted and avoiding Lida's eyes, added, 'If only all our members had such a responsible attitude.'

'Quite right, Mrs Mackey,' Ginny said, keeping a straight face in the face of Lida's feigned look of indignation.

With one last squeeze of their handshake, they parted ways and made for their respective base lines. Lida looked over her shoulder to where Tommy stood and to her surprise saw that her mother's place had been taken by Hubert. Instinctively, her eyes were drawn to the bench where Rose sat. Anna Hendel had joined her, and the two mothers were shaking hands.

Both Ginny and Lida paused at the same time and glanced at each other with equal disbelief. When she reached her base line, Lida swung her racket getting the feel of that heavier weight again. She looked up and her father was there, standing behind Tommy and Hubert. Their eyes met as they'd done in the garden at Garravicleheen but there was no longer any distance between them. He raised his thumb and looked around him proudly at the hushed, expectant audience. The calm was dissipating into sudden coughs and solitary, echoing exhortations – the loudest coming from Mags.

'Come on, Lida,' and, as if to maintain the balance of favour, 'Come on, Ginny!'

The storm was about to begin and Lida prayed they would both survive – with their friendship intact.

'Miss Hendel to serve,' Mrs Mackey declared, basking in her role as club secretary, umpire, organiser – the one without whom, in her own mind, none of this would have been possible.

The ball sprang back into Lida's fist, once, twice, bouncing up from the newly-trimmed grass. She threw it above her and Ginny, crouching at the far end, swayed to her right. Before Lida could summon the strength in her arms, aching from tension, the ball was at her feet again and she looked apologetically to Ginny. But Ginny's eyes were on the ball and she noticed nothing of Lida's hesitancy. Mrs Mackey regarded Lida crossly and she tried again. Her delivery was good and the pace of it was too much for Ginny.

This, her first score, an ace, brought forth a smattering of applause that seemed to clear the air, for the moment, of its high-pitched expectancy. Her next service struck the fine-tuned line of the net cord and rang out a false, muted note on the metal stanchions to each side. The second service stayed in and, though Ginny got to it, there was no power in her return and Lida dispatched it safely with a cross-court volley. Thirty-love.

Ginny's next return was more positive and Lida, failing to get herself behind it quickly enough, had to let it pass by her to bounce a hair's breadth inside the line. This brief lapse stirred her and she held her next two service shots and took the game.

With the first loud grunt of the afternoon, Ginny too began with an ace. In fact, she began with three aces, each emphasised with a more explosive release of breath than the one before.

On the fourth serve, Lida caught her rushing the net and lobbed her expertly for the point – the only point she won in that second game.

Stuck fast to their base lines now, they battled out the

third game, point for point, until a top-spin volley didn't quite come off for Lida and she found herself trailing at 30–40 in her own service game. Instead of playing safe, she went for the kill on her second service and was sure the ball brushed off the net before landing beyond the tram lines.

'Net!' she cried.

'Out! Game to Miss Stannix,' Mrs Mackey retorted. 'And no antics please, Miss Hendel.'

Lida looked to Ginny and tried to believe that her friend would have supported her if it had really been a net ball. It was easy, she knew, to imagine these things in the heat of play. She urged herself to stop making excuses. The net was there to be played over and that was all there was to it.

Now, Ginny was playing a short game, touching shots in over the net and trying to draw Lida out into the forecourt. She wasn't to be drawn but neither was she reaching the stop-shots slamming tantalisingly into the grass before her. This time she failed to register a single score and the match stood at 3–1 to Ginny.

A chance to towel away the perspiration and rest came at last. Among the spectators, conversation drowned out conversation, but Lida and Ginny couldn't even bring themselves to look at each other. As Lida prepared to serve again the urging, surging crowd seemed to press in on her, demanding a better show.

Succumbing to nerves, Lida's play became ragged. Her carefully thought-out plan to change her tactics subtly as the game went on came to pieces. The idea had been to alternate between rushing the net and sticking to the base line on successive shots at this critical point in the match. However, she lost track of when she was supposed to do which and, more often than not, found herself floundering in the no-man's land in between.

Four–1 down, Lida faced Ginny's service again with fading confidence. The noises coming from the once quietly elegant girl were becoming intolerable. Leading 30–love, Ginny was beaten by a crisp snap-shot return of Lida's and let it by disgustedly, only to see it come to ground a half-inch beyond the line.

'Bad luck, Lida,' she called without thinking.

Lida was incensed but staunched the flow of invective boiling up within her. The frown below her dark fringe was enough warning for Ginny. It didn't happen again but the hint of pity drove Lida to greater efforts.

One malicious shot after another rained down on Ginny until she caved in entirely and lost her service with a passing shot that should have been easy to make but was badly fluffed. Four–2. Lida went on to hold her own service in the face of Ginny's mounting rage.

The ill-humoured ferocity with which Ginny brought the set to 5–3 in her favour was frightening to behold. She threw down the Blue Flash she'd been using until now and, picking up its twin, proceeded to batter Lida's backhand with cruelly swerving shots that proved un-answerable. Instead of the encouraging calls to Lida, her game was peppered with curses which Mrs Mackey chose to ignore.

The last game of the set saw Lida in even deeper trouble. Shots that might have been aces against any other player were returned with even greater pace than they were delivered.

She felt like an entrenched solider who, every time he raises his head above the parapet, is met with a volley of sniper fire. Surrender seemed the only way out and surrender the game and the set was what Lida was forced to do.

Crossing close by each other, they exchanged looks that were momentarily frosty. Ginny, calmer now that the heat was off her, was moved to offer an explanation.

'I wasn't cursing at you, Lida,' she said and Lida, remembering when her own game was littered with noisy outbursts, knew she'd let herself misunderstand Ginny in the same way as everyone else had misunderstood her old self.

'I know,' Lida said.

From among the crowd, the familiar voice of a young boy exploded and a wave of unspoken shame seemed to dull the spectators' conversations.

'Go on, Stannix! Crucify her!'

It was the red-haired fellow who'd felt the fury of Lida's service when she'd played Mags. Those around him moved a step away and left him standing, red-faced and sheepish, alone in his naked hatred. Ginny was so upset that she moved towards the boy with vengeance in her eyes. Lida held her back.

'Leave him,' she said and, dispirited, they went their separate ways into the small rectangular world of grassy earth, bounded by the white lines that marked the border between success and failure.

The large gathering seemed somehow to have retreated and Lida felt much less aware of their menacing presence. Ginny, too, had pulled herself back from the brink and the match entered a quieter, more tentative phase. Both girls held service without great difficulty in the space of a lacklustre twenty minutes until at 4–4 in the second set, Ginny committed a glaring error.

At deuce in the ninth game, Lida returned Ginny's serve with a whipped top-spin forehand drive that came undone as soon as it left her racket. The ball rose invitingly within Ginny's reach at the forecourt. Lida, scrambling to change direction, lost her footing and lay at Ginny's mercy. To the collective astonishment of the crowd, Ginny missed the gaping hole between the lines on Lida's side and sent the ball high into the next field.

Ginny's next service was a poor one and Lida, with the minimum of effort, pushed it wide of her stranded opponent. Five–4 to Lida.

The spectators inching forward once more, Lida knew she'd reached a point of no return in the match and the knowledge infected her service with a leaden hamfistedness. Her timid shots, however, were more than adequate to confound a disconsolate Ginny. It was clear that if Lida lost this game, it would be through her own fault.

She held on, despite giving away two ridiculously easy points. Six–4: the set was hers. All that dogged concentration and sweating effort had been expended for nothing. They were back to where they started. Or so it seemed.

As the third set got under way, everyone there could see that the battle had taken a greater toll on Ginny than it had on Lida. The loss of her service in the first game, it seemed to Lida, proved that the fight was going out of her opponent and friend. Cannonball deliveries and gravity-defying returns saw Lida gain two successive love games and a comprehensive lead of 3–0.

Now, Ginny's silence was worse than her former antics. The last thing Lida wanted was to see her friend giving in or, as she began to suspect, offering an easy victory in return for what Lida had done for her. If she was going to win, she wanted no shadows cast on that victory.

In the fourth game with Lida serving, Ginny came close to keeping in a return and Lida saw her chance.

'Unlucky!' she called and Ginny, suddenly woken from her dead air of submission, responded with a fiery look.

When she gained her first point in the game with Mrs Mackey's help, Ginny's arousal was complete.

'Out!' the club secretary yelped after a service which Lida knew she hadn't hit well, though she couldn't see exactly where it had bounced.

'It was in,' Ginny said, aggrieved at being shown favour.

Mrs Mackey, whose temper had been sorely tested by Lida's surging lead, banged her little fists together in exasperation.

'I am the umpire, Miss Stannix,' she said. 'Miss Hendel, get on with it.'

Revitalised, Ginny clawed her way back into the game and soon had Lida regretting her goading tactic. A pair of remarkable returns, both hit while she was impossibly off-balance, saw her break Lida's serve and a string of deliberately struck aces ensured her own following service game stayed intact. Three–2 and the initiative had returned once more to Ginny.

In a tense, belligerent sixth game, points were swapped with increasing vigour right down to deuce. Lida's service was faltering and an air of bad feeling between the two opponents threatened to spill over into words at the slightest provocation.

Lida tried desperately to turn her anger from Ginny and, one after another, she remembered the faces of her tormentors and levelled silent accusations against them: Mrs Mackey, cheating her at every turn; the stupid red-haired boy; Rose Stannix and her despicable letter; Tommy, refusing to support her in her attempts to take matters in hand at Garravicleheen; her father, putting her through so much anguish before she'd got what she'd wanted.

Wanting. Wanting. Her favourite word, Lida thought, as she missed yet another angled volley from Ginny. A new racket, a new dress, a new house. As if any of these things really mattered when all was said and done. She wasn't playing badly now for the want of a new racket. Hadn't she won the second set with this one? And the new house? What guarantee was that of happiness? If a nice house guaranteed happiness, then life should have been perfect at Stannix House.

Another shot fudged and she wondered what getting the new house entailed for her father. Years' more labour to make the payments? Or was it more positive than that? Did it just show that the battle of life went on and you worked hard for every small pleasure and made your own luck on the way? In the end, moving to Slievebawn meant, most importantly, that her father had raised his sights from the blinkered vision of the past and, in turn, had rescued all of them from despair.

Wanting. Wanting. And after all the wanting, she knew she had something Ginny could never have now. A living, breathing father to love, to talk to, to help her through the bad times. All at once, her anger had evaporated. The game was won and she felt a new calm. Three–3, the set stood, and Tommy's worried voice rang in her ears.

'Come on, Lida,' he shouted but the words she heard, though still Tommy's, were different.

'No perfect endings.' And she shuddered with the force of Ginny's shot meeting her own racket.

'Shut up, Tommy,' she muttered. 'No, I mean, shut up, Lida.'

An exquisite quietude descended on her as she blotted all thoughts from her mind and faced Ginny's second service. The battle of individual wills was slowly raised to something much greater. Both girls had reached such a depth of concentration, such a height of skill, that the tennis they played became a thing of beauty in itself. Sustained rallies, strokes of brilliance and counterstrokes of amazing quality had the spectators in a delirium of admiration.

Their service games became, for a while, impregnable, even if neither one had more than a point to spare in holding on. Four–4. Five–5. When Lida broke service in the next game it wasn't by default but through two strokes of absolute genius. The first was a return of Ginny's lob which Lida hit overhead as she raced away, her back to the net. The second was a low ground shot, scooped from below the net, which inched its way over the cord and dropped like a stone on the other side. Six–5 to Lida.

The pressure on her next service game was intense. Ginny, unperturbed by the miraculous shots of the previous game, pulled back each and every point Lida had won. At deuce, they continued to match each other until the service reverted to Ginny.

Not a whisper rose from the phalanx of onlookers as Ginny laid up the ball for this vital serve. The anguished protest of the struck net cord was all the louder for the silence. Second serve. Ginny wasn't taking chances and the power of the shot wasn't good enough to beat Lida, whose return was decisive.

Ginny tried again. And again the first serve met the net. And again it fell back into her forecourt. Now, she was playing to save the match. Her racket rose in a wide sweeping arc to meet the dropping ball. Lida dived to her right but the ball went by her – and crashed to the ground, outside the line.

There was a stunned silence. Lida wanted someone to cheer so she'd know for certain she hadn't imagined the ball was out. And then she didn't want them to cheer because now she could see Ginny's face and she knew she'd been right. When Mrs Mackey spoke, Lida was thrown into further confusion.

'Net!' was the cry, followed by an intake of breath from the crowd.

Lida dusted off her white skirt and stared at the grass, quelling the wave of protest rising in her throat. She tried to remember the ball's flight after it had left Ginny's racket but the net cord refused to sing its distress into her mind.

It hadn't been a net ball. Nothing could convince her that it had been. She looked up, at last, to face the second service and saw Ginny walking towards the umpire. The blonde girl didn't seem at all disappointed and her smile, the one Lida had so distrusted in the past, seemed as sincere as it was knowing.

'The ball never touched the net, Mrs Mackey,' Ginny said.

Mrs Mackey squirmed as if aware that the attention of everyone in the grounds had fallen on her and found her wanting.

'Really, Miss Stannix,' she said, and Lida could see that for the first time, she'd lost patience with Ginny; more than that, there was a hint of her true feelings for Ginny and all the Stannixes. 'Rule 14(c), the decisions of the umpire will at all times be respected. There are no exceptions to that rule.'

'It didn't touch the net,' Ginny repeated, 'and it was out.'

Turning dismissively from the outraged Mrs Mackey, Ginny reached her hand across the net. Still rooted to her base line, Lida knew that she could accept that hand without misgivings since she'd won the match fairly. She could also, however, give Ginny a second chance and that, in its own way, might be fair too. One way or the other, there was no doubt that if the match went on, Ginny was as likely to win as Lida and, right now, Lida wouldn't have minded.

Mrs Mackey sat down, silenced, defeated. The crowd grew restive. Though standing yards apart from one another, both girls knew they had wrested this match from Mrs Mackey and from the crowd. What happened next was down to them and they simply had to look at each other to know what to decide. But the decision wasn't easy for either of them, and they hesitated for what seemed like an eternity.

CHAPTER 21

Ger Kinsella, resplendent in a red tuxedo, his sparse tuft of hair greased back, stood at the microphone. One hand was slung casually in his pocket, the other whipped the band along on its bouncing ride through the music's rhythm. In the soft light of a packed Parnell Hall, his transformation was complete. The very skin of his time-scarred face bloomed with an ease and confidence that was reflected in the deep lushness of his singing voice.

To his left, Tommy Hendel played as if possessed. The old piano, its front still pock-marked from bullets fired twenty-six years before during the Civil War, was holding up well to this new, more innocent, assault. Despite the age difference, he and Ger were like brothers in music, happiest on the real home of all musicians – the stage.

The drummer clashed his cymbals; a saxophone snaked its smooth passage of melody; a trumpet blew out high exclamations as if in wonder at the coming together of sounds; and beneath the dancers, the dusty boards reverberated with the big heartbeat of the dance.

Lida, in her new green shot taffeta dress from Dempsey's, spun away from Ginny and dizzily caught her hand again. The startling vision of Ginny's scarlet dress made her even more light-headed. In fact, everything about this night added more to her sense of exhilaration and release.

Her parents sat at the far end of the hall sharing a table with Rose and Hubert Stannix. They talked and took turns dancing with each other and the initial embarrassment that Lida had felt watching her parents waltzing together soon passed. Her mother seemed to have left her shyness outside the ballroom door and her father, decked out in his best – his only – suit, looked just as young and carefree as Tommy did on the stage. Rose and Hubert danced with even more polished grace than they'd done in the study at Stannix House.

Ever since Lida had arrived at eight o'clock and met Ginny and Mags, people had been coming over to congratulate them on the best display of tennis seen at the club for years. No one, not even Mags, mentioned winners or losers. It was the game of tennis, they all agreed, which had won out on the day.

But for Lida, Ginny, Mags and all the other junior members, the night was nearing its end. Mrs Mackey wasn't about to bend any rules and they would, as always, be leaving after the presentation of the trophies. The dance would go on until one o'clock but Lida didn't mind. She and her two friends had their own plans. They were all staying at Stannix House at the invitation of Rose Stannix.

As Lida and Ginny made their way back to the table where Mags was resting from her earlier exertions on the dance floor, Mrs Mackey's voice crackled in over the microphone.

'Is this thing working, Mr Kinsella?' she whispered and hearing her own words fill the hall she jumped back to the amusement of all those watching.

She stiffened up primly as a few sniggers raised themselves above the hum of conversation.

'Yes? Well, ladies and gentlemen,' she announced. 'We've come to the big moment of the evening. The first trophy I shall present is to the Junior Girls Champion ...'

Behind her, the drummer raised his sticks and made ready to bang out a crescendo.

'And this year's champion, as you all know by now, is ...'

The drumsticks descended too quickly and the name was lost in the crashing roll of noise and the ear-splitting round of hand-clapping that followed.

Darkness hadn't yet fallen as they drove, on that summer night in 1948, towards Stannix House. Hubert's humming filled the exhausted silence that had come over Lida, Ginny and Mags. The silver cup with its new tab on the ebony black base rested on Mag's lap. Its huge importance, its terrible hold over Lida and Ginny, had cleared just as surely as the ghosts of their parents' past had done. They were at peace and nothing could disturb that tired but comfortable feeling. Not even Hubert's unexpected announcement.

'The house is sold,' he said and the words flowed so naturally out of the tune he was humming that it seemed now a thing of little consequence.

'Who's bought it?' Lida asked quietly.

'How does Mackey House sound to you?' Ginny asked and, for the first time, Lida realised that strangers now lived in that farmhouse in Moravia she had always imagined as an empty shell waiting for their return; and knew that it didn't matter who those people were, any more than it mattered who would now live in Stannix House.

Hubert steered carefully along the drive into Stannix House. Under the canopy of vast oak trees darkening the passage, he switched on the headlamps. Before them, the House, suddenly lit up, seemed achingly beautiful in its rustic red splendour. Out of the shade, he turned off the lights again and the place was, somehow, quite ordinary once more, its red bricks faded with a chalky whiteness, the paint on the window arches blistered and peeling.

At the front door, they piled out of the car and, with a last wave, Hubert drove away to enjoy the rest of the dance. Mags held out the trophy like it was some burdensome boulder.

'I'm fed up of lugging this thing around all evening,' she said cheerfully. 'You should be carrying it. It's yours.'

Neither Ginny nor Lida moved to take possession of it. In the distance, the birds were singing the last songs of the evening and coming home to rest among the trees that had stood for a hundred years and would stand for a hundred years more.

At last, Ginny took the trophy and passed her fingers along the silver that should have been cold but had been warmed in Mags's hold.

'Maybe we should have played on after that double-fault, Ginny. Maybe it wasn't a double-fault at all,' Lida said, but Ginny shook her head and presented the trophy to her with more grace and sincerity than Mrs Mackey had done in the Parnell Hall.

And they went inside and closed the door
on the night. And the lightest wisp of a breeze
passed through the Swinging Tree and was gone,
silent as the smoke from a garden barrel,
silent as the cloud that passes to reveal the stars.

ALSO FROM WOLFHOUND PRESS

MELODY FOR NORA

Mark O'Sullivan

**WINNER OF THE EILÍS DILLON MEMORIAL AWARD,
BISTO BOOK OF THE YEAR**

Nora is a survivor – and music is her lifeline.
The Civil War has just begun – the times are explosive
and threatening. Nora's life is changed by her mother's
tragic illness and a drunken father who cannot cope. She
is sent to an aunt and uncle in Tipperary who
may as well be strangers.

Here to her surprise is a cinema, and an eccentric
piano-player, Alec, with a haunting melody. And here
Nora finds herself forced to play an unexpected role in
the unfolding intrigues and conflicts of her time.

Melody for Nora is a powerful novel of heartbreak in a
troubled family, of living through civil war, and of a
young girl's extraordinary resourcefulness.

'An unusual and imaginative read.'
Books Ireland

ISBN 0 86327 425 0

WASH-BASIN STREET BLUES

Mark O'Sullivan

The omens are foreboding, even crossing the Atlantic.
Whose is the frightening face pressed against the
window as Nora plays the grand piano aboard ship?
Why does she distrust her new aunt Fay?
Just who is betraying who?

Here is a mystery she must solve. A metallic clanging
sound disturbs Nora's dreams, turning them into
nightmares. A net of fear and violence is closing in.
Must she buy into the New York criminal underworld?
It seems to be her only choice . . .

As the emotional storms brew, Nora faces a moral
dilemma that demands courage, honesty and personal
change if her family is to be saved.

ISBN 0 86327 467 6

ALSO FROM WOLFHOUND PRESS

The Sandclocker
Jack Scoltock

A historical adventure set at the time of the Spanish
Armada, this is the story of two cousins, Diego and Tomas,
who run away to sea to fight the English. Life on board the
Trinidad Valencera is vividly described – scurvy, seasick-
ness, lice and canon fire. The boys fear for their lives in
storm after storm and raging sea battles. Gripping stuff
written by one of the divers who discovered the Armada
wreckage off the coast of Kinnago Bay in 1971.

ISBN 0 86327 531 1

A Girl and a Dolphin
Patrick O'Sullivan

What would it be like to see a real wild dolphin? Anna
finds out when an unexpected visitor swims into her secret
cove – a bottle nosed dolphin! As the summer slips by,
their unusual friendship grows.

But the local fishermen don't want unwelcome guests in
their waters, and Donal's diving for sunken treasure must
remain undisturbed. In a story full of drama and
adventure, Patrick O'Sullivan captures all the magic of a
wild creature living close to humans.

Inspired by Fungi the Dingle dolphin

ISBN 0 86327 426 9

ALSO FROM WOLFHOUND PRESS

Cinderella's Fella

Aislinn O'Loughlin

You're a Prince named Fred, but Dad the King calls you
'Charming'. Now he wants you to hold a ball. And find
yourself a wife. Things just can't get any worse. Or can
they? Enter wobbly Priscilla and screeching Rosemary.
And exit the best-looking girl at the ball – in a midnight
disappearing act. But help is at hand as Prince Fred's sis-
ters and friends come to the rescue (backwards on a horse!)
The surprising and hilarious story of Cinderella – from a
guy who was really there.

A first book by fourteen-year-old author
Aislinn O'Loughlin
'A very funny book.' *RTE Guide*
'A hilarious reworking of the familiar tale.' *Sunday Tribune*
ISBN 0 86327 493 5

A Right Royal Pain

Aislinn O'Loughlin

Rumpelstiltskin: The True Story
When Rummy's best friend Shakademus (the Blackbird
with the BIG voice), tells him that the miller's daughter is
in trouble, Rummy decides to help her out. He expects to
get some funny looks becuase of his, er, um . . . unusual
appearance. But what he doesn't expect is – being taken for
granted by a right royal pain; having an unwanted baby
land on his doorstep; and becoming the villain of the piece
– when all he was trying to do is lend a helping hand.
ISBN 0 86327 514 1

FORTHCOMING TITLES

Up The Red Belly
Margot Bosonnet

The Red Belly gang are on the rampage. Follow them on
their hair-raising escapades involving a scary night in a
haunted house and wrecking a vegetable garden with a
dog-drawn home-made chariot! Gripping, exciting and
comical stuff full of fun and irreverence. Will appeal to
children of seven onwards.

ISBN 0 86327 530 3

The Silver Chalice
Shelagh Jones

A local museum visit for eleven-year-old Paul Sheehan is
the beginning of a time travel trip of a lifetime, but exactly
whose life time is not so clear. Involving distraught monks,
modern day biker Vikings, a stubborn pig called Tantony
and a lost chalice at the heart of the search, Paul tries to
unravel a mess that's over one thousand years old! For
readers of eight up.

ISBN 0 86327 540 0